RAW IMAGE

Behind the Lens Mysteries
Book One

By Laurie Fagen

Published by
Change It Up Press
Chandler, AZ

ISBN: 978-1-968694-11-1

Library of Congress Control Number: 2025920197

Published by Change It Up Press
A division of www.ReadLaurieFagen.com
Chandler, AZ

Cover design by Tad Smith
Book Shepherd Ann Videan, ANVidean.com

This book is dedicated to Jessica C. Williams, a longtime friend,
former Women in Communications, Inc. colleague, Spa Girlz organizer,
cookbook author and Talk Story partner.

We've always been each other's writing and business cheerleaders,
and Jess is the one who came up with
the "Behind the Lens" name for this new series.

Love you, my friend!

Chapter 1

The blinking light in my video camera's viewfinder is a soothing sign of control, function, performance.

The graphic footage I'm shooting of 32 bloodied people after being brutally slaughtered is not.

Compose. Focus.

Wide shot of body after dead body, sprawled on the gleaming tile shopping mall floor in unnatural silent positions—some by themselves, some clumped with others—fill the eyepiece of my trusty Sony FS9 camera. I zoom in on a blood-spattered purse, lying agape, where lipstick, pens, cough drops and other items have spilled out. Another close-up view of a man's dress shoe, tipped on its side, no owner nearby. *Tilt up.* The monitor fills with Albuquerque, New Mexico's signature hot air balloon as it hangs limply from the high domed ceiling, several holes blasted through it. Multiple cell phones ring, never to be answered again.

In this new world of monthly or more mass shootings and the government's inability to legislate any change, the media argued the way to force decisions might be to broadcast portions of the bloodshed. And they won.

Which makes my job easier.

The metallic smell of blood mixed with urine and sweat does not.

Another tight shot of a child's pink pacifier. Next to a stroller. *Not a baby!* I turn my face away from the lens to hastily search around for a little one. I don't see a child among the fallen, and in relief, blow out the air held momentarily in my lungs. *Hopefully she got away with her parents.*

Careful not to show any faces of the dead, I continue my work as a freelance video journalist—and do my best to tamp down my own emotions—as I record the gruesome crime scene while glum police officers, crime scene techs, emergency medical personnel and other select media toil somberly inside the Albuquerque Fashion Center. Outside, armed guards protect the building's perimeter, where I already shot footage of the few who made it out with a pulse.

Previously an upscale shopping mall, it would now and forever be known as the site of another one of the largest mass shootings in the country. Chances are it will be torn down, as no one will ever want to buy from any store there again. Huge losses for the business owners, not to mention the entire center itself, which—

An electronic voice in my cell phone earpiece identifies a caller: Always Online Digital News assignment desk. *Now what? They always call at the worst times.*

"Answer."

"TJ? You still there? I need that footage A-SAP," barks a female voice.

Bitch, I'll get it to you when I get it to you. I stop taping and lower the camera, trying not to breathe in the smell of death. "I am in the mall, shooting the shooting victims." A dramatic pause for the sick pun. "Give me five minutes."

"Oh. Sorry. Ok. Thanks." A click, and gratefully the voice is gone.

Cable news will only be allowed to televise certain shots of the lifeless bodies, so I videotape close-ups where a person can't be identified, then turn my attention to the first responders.

I'm one of only a few videographers always available for hire and seemingly impervious to the blood and gore in scenes like these, thanks to the invisible shield I surround myself with to help protect my psyche. Some say that makes me appear cold, but it's how I keep my reactions and emotions in check while on the job.

I've covered crime and accident scenes starting at the local TV market level, moving up to regional and now national news assignments. *The bigger the assignment, the larger the body count, the thicker my wall.*

The term "MMJ" or "multi-media journalist" was my title when I started in this crazy business some 15 years ago, but it's not my favorite. Oh, I can shoot, edit, write a good story and do stand-ups with the best of them. But I don't need my face or even my voice on the report. I just want to tell stories with video and soundbites, what producers call "natural sound stories" or nat/sot—natural sound on tape—pieces. They're actually harder to create than those with pre-written voiceovers, because you have to have exactly the right interviews and enough natural sound to tell the story without narration. But I know the questions to ask to solicit the best soundbites.

"Time's up, Banks." A curt, deep voice comes up from behind me. I pan the camera around to catch "L. Sereno" on a gold Albuquerque Police Department badge before tilting the lens up to frame the officer's ruddy brown face. *The things he's probably seen.* The many hours spent on drive-alongs with cops remind me we share a similar trait: the ability to compartmentalize. Partially to keep us as objective as is possible, and mostly to attempt to protect our mental health in an otherwise gritty world of crime.

"Got it." I stop recording. "Any word on the shooter?"

"No, not yet." Sereno works his jaw back and forth. "Somehow he caused all this carnage and managed to escape."

"Good luck." Wavering between shooting one last video or escaping from the horrendous death scene, I slip off the blue protective booties, toss them in a bin and walk out into the bright New Mexico spring sunshine.

Chapter 2

U sed to be, the most depraved crimes occurred between 2 and 4 a.m., after the bars closed and idiots ran amok, juiced up on booze.

Predictable. Expected.

Now, yet another mass shooting, taking place in the middle of the morning, in the middle of the workweek, in the middle of a crowded mall.

You never know. Could be anyplace, anytime.

I shake my head in disgust at the senseless crime. *Is this what my job has come to?* I slide off the backwards baseball cap smashing my short, jet black hair and ruffle my fingers through it to spike it up again.

The initial raw footage is uploaded to the assignment editor at AODN, or Always Online Digital News, so they can use it immediately for their "breaking news" segments. The sun is warm on my face as I search through the crowd of onlookers standing behind yellow and black crime scene tape, flapping in the soft breeze. *They're gonna want soundbites from survivors, witnesses, cops, just about anyone.* The building is surrounded by a blue sea of armed local law enforcement personnel. Five red-and-white ambulances, lined up and ready to take the injured to area hospitals, get no business.

I spot a young woman holding a crying baby, attempting to talk to a police officer over its wails. I casually saunter over within hearing distance. *Is she a witness?* I pick up snatches of the woman's voice: "bunch of pop, pop, pop sounds," and "then I ran."

I want that soundbite. No blood, so she wasn't hit. But chances are good she'll be emotionally scarred for a long time to come. I continue to listen as the adrenaline begins to pulse in my heart.

The officer finishes his interrogation and leaves. The barely 20-something female stands there, looking lost for a moment, unable to console her child. I put my camera back in its bag and approach her carefully.

"'Scuse me, I'm with AOD News. Were you inside during the shooting?"

The woman's head swings toward me, her large brown eyes wide with surprise. "Yes, and I just told the police everything." She starts to walk away.

"Wait." I dig in my pocket and pull out the pacifier, the faint scent of baby powder clinging to it. The memory of the crime scene tech's weary, grief-stricken face flashes through my mind. He hadn't hesitated when I urged him to process it immediately, so I think he, too, recognized this small comfort needed to be reconciled with the little one who must be missing it.

"Is this your baby's?" I ask, holding out the pink rubber plug decorated with butterflies.

The young mother stares in disbelief for a moment, then grabs it. She brushes it quickly on her blue jeans and pops it in her still-anguished little girl's mouth. The crying stops, and the baby's eyes close, long eyelashes and chubby little face wet with tears.

"Thanks." The woman's thin shoulders relax, her collar and shoulder bones protruding sharply from a turquoise tank top. Her mousy brown locks have been hastily thrust up with a clip, and now several pieces of stringy hair are escaping, falling around her pale face. She sighs, and I can sense her relief.

"Do you need to sit down for a few minutes?" I gesture toward a concrete bench, a small tree with a bit of shade. "I'll find you something to drink."

The girl nods silently as I grab two cold plastic bottles of water from an ice chest set up by a local community group. I hand a couple of dollar bills to the volunteer and start to walk away.

"They're free. You don't have to pa—" The man's voice trails off as I flick my hand to disregard his comment and down a third of the liquid, as I try to wash away the taste of death. I head back to the young woman and her now quiet child.

I open the other bottle and hand it to her. "I'm TJ. What's your name?"

"Thanks." The girl takes a sip. "I'm Barbara Hopkins, but you can call me Barbie. This is Eva."

The baby's red, sweaty head snuggles on her mother's shoulder, and she's fast asleep, sucking the pacifier.

"Was that your stroller inside as well?"

"Oh my god, it is!" Barbie starts to stand, then stops, not wanting to wake her child. "And my cell phone!"

Bingo.

"I've got to get it. Will they let me in?" Barbie's voice is panicky.

"I'm media. Let me try. You stay here." The young mother's face melts into a look of thankfulness.

Chapter 3

I'm able to talk my way back into the crime scene, accurately describing the baby stroller and maybe not so accurately what else was in it. I'm granted permission to take it to the young mom.

The second trip allows me to count the number of victims once again. Same tally: 32. No one had been moved since my first time in, and the stench invading my sensitive nose now includes feces and vomit. I wrap a bandana around my nose and mouth to mask the smell.

The occasional ring tone chirps from a mobile phone, then ends. I try to tune out the still-playing, inane overhead music, an easy-listening cover of some old '80s song.

Careful where I step, I spot the cell in the buggy seat and casually toss a baby blanket over it. I push it out into the cleaner air and back to where Barbie sits.

"Oh, thank you so much!" She digs under the blanket to pick up the phone with one hand, the other still cradling the sleeping child. "I don't even remember throwing it down to pick up Eva. I just knew I had to get outta there, and it would be faster running without the stroller."

"Did you videotape any of it?" I ask casually. *Even better than a witness soundbite.*

"Actually, yeah. Don't laugh—"

"Oh, I won't. Sorry, but may I record?" I interrupt, pulling my camera out of the bag.

Barbie's eyebrows furrow. "Wait, you one of those TV people?"

"Yeah, AOD News, remember? What were you going to say? And I promise I won't laugh." I smile and bring the viewfinder back up to my right eye. *Red light blinking. Nice tight close-up.*

The young woman pauses a moment, then continues. "Well, at first I thought it was one of those, ya know, flash mob thingies. This guy starts singing, something about 'I love my country, the USA,' so I start videoing and kept looking for others to join him. Then all of a sudden…" Barbie's voice chokes, remembering. "He pulls out this huge gun and starts shooting… " She tightly embraces the baby as tears run down her face.

About 20 seconds. Gold.

I lower my camera. "It must've been horrible," I say softly, and hold out my hand toward the phone. "May I?" Barbie gives it to me, sniffling.

I pull up the last video shot and press play. The rest of the refrain continues, sung in a powerful tenor voice: "But I won't give it over to the Jews who betray."

Double gold.

"Who is he?" Barbie asks in a husky voice.

"Probably a white supremacist. He… got away, so you ought to head straight home. Um, did you tell the police about the video?" *I hope not.*

"I totally forgot. I was so scared. Am I gonna get in trouble?"

"No, I wouldn't worry about it. But may I send this video to myself? It might help identify the shooter." *And nab me a major bonus for having footage of the perp. Triple gold.*

"Sure, go ahead." She gently lays the sleeping baby in the stroller as I upload the footage to my phone.

I dig into my pocket and pull out cash and a business card. "Thanks. Call me if you remember anything else, or just wanna talk. And here's a little something for the video." I press a bill into Barbie's hand with my contact info and head out. Glancing back, I smile at the young mom's look of surprise as she discovers $100.

Chapter 4

I make another pass around the exterior of the massive mall, and look for anything suspicious, but assume the shooter is long gone.

The crowd has grown to include frantic family members and the curious. They huddle in small groups, some crying, some stoic, some whispering amongst themselves. I could get more interviews, but I'm anxious to study Barbie's footage closer. I want to run it through facial and voice recognition software and only then, maybe share it with police or FBI.

A text message notification dings. I pull out my phone. It's Roger Lester, the assignment editor from News Crews International who finds many of my TV news gigs.

Still in ABQ? he writes.

Yes prolly rest of day.

Another ding. *You OK?*

I pause a moment before responding. Normally I'd automatically send a "thumbs up" emoji, but a wave of fatigue hits me. I squeeze my eyes shut and rub one hand over them. *I've got a potential scoop over everyone, but I'm suddenly beat. After 15 years, is this what I want to keep doing? The job used to be more exciting. Is there something else that would bring a different satisfaction? Maybe…* The phone in my hand rings, and I jump. Caller ID says "Roger."

"Too long, TJ. What's up?" Roger's smooth baritone voice is a another one of the very few comforting things in my life.

"Jeez, Rog, I can't have 10 seconds?"

"I know you, girl. One of the fastest texters on the team. You okay?"

I want to avoid that subject. "Why, you got another job for me?"

"Always. You're the number one request. But don't ignore my question. What's wrong?"

Damn, he knows me too well. We met while working at CNN in Atlanta, and as my producer, we were practically joined at the hip for a couple of years. Gave us lots of time for deep conversations, plenty of laughs, even a brief "friends with benefits" trial. The pang in my heart reminds me how much I miss those times.

But since I went freelance and he went to NCI, sending video crews around the world, all that changed. Now, in the fast-paced news biz, there's little time for self-reflection, not to mention relationships.

"More of the same old, same old. Days like these… so many dead people… maybe I need to get a different life."

"You want me to find other gigs for you?" The sound of rustling papers comes through the phone, and I can imagine him working remotely in his trendy penthouse apartment in Atlanta, three computer screens, desk full of files. "Let's see… I've got a big wind turbine dispute between residents and businesses in Iowa… there are always women's issues in Saudi… or what about—"

"Nah, that's not really it either. I don't know… look, I wanna keep working this story for now. I think it's going to explode. Take me out of rotation for a few days, okay?"

"Sure, but what's bigger than 32 people dead?"

"The shooter on tape."

"Whoa, seriously? Hey, just remember who got you this job, okay? Keep me posted. And TJ…" Roger pauses. "I'm always here if you wanna talk, you know that, right?"

"Sure. Thanks."

"And TJ, you *can* let others in more often."

Back in my hotel room, I send the video from my phone to my laptop and start the facial recognition software.

The search will take a while, so I strip off my black T-shirt, black leather boots, black jeans and bikini underwear, stuff them in a plastic laundry sack and head to the shower. I scrub, from head to toe three times, hard, attempting to wash off the odor of blood and death.

Thoughts swirl through my head. *Do I need a change of assignments? Do I need a whole new job? But what would I do? This is all I know.* I flash back on my first TV position in a small market in Alabama, where everyone would go out to dinner or for drinks at the end of the week. *Is that what's missing? Camaraderie? Girlfriends? A steady relationship?* Not easy to do in this nomadic lifestyle of traveling to a different state every few days.

And what did Roger mean about "letting others in more often?" I let him in just this morning. *For a few minutes. Oh.*

So, that may be part of it. But there's something else. I can't quite figure it out yet.

I dry off and swipe the foggy mirror with the towel to clear a spot. My hand gently caresses the small diamond hanging from a gold chain around my neck, remembering its giver with a smile. I run my fingers through my wet, cropped hair, creating my signature all-over, feisty spikes. My version of "styling." Refreshed by the hot water, I catch my pale blue eyes in the reflection, looking weary, sad.

"Buck up, kid. You can sleep when you're dead."

I dress in a fresh black T-shirt and black jeans, make a pot of hotel coffee and turn back to the computer.

Chapter 5

You're a genius. A fucking genius.

Patrick Newberry's breathing slows as he stretches on a chaise lounge in his boxers next to someone's beautiful blue pool. His clothes and weapon are hidden in his backpack, and he tries hard to look like a guy just chillin' on a warm day. He hopes the owners won't come home anytime soon.

No one will ever find me here. Unless they send out those damned dogs. Did he leave anything that could give them a scent? No, he was much too careful for that.

Could really use a beer. Maybe the jerks who were stupid enough to leave the backyard gate unlocked would leave a door or window the same way. *Better not. Don't want to get arrested for a stupid B&E after pulling off his greatest achievement ever.*

Patrick's heart pounds again as he relives the shooting. He can still feel the solid metal of the AR-15 in his hands, the rapid firing and recoil of each bullet jerking his arms. The burst of adrenaline rushing through his chest and head while mowing down all those rich white snobs. He just kept spraying those AR bad boy cartridges back and forth. He flexes his right fingers, remembering. *Wait 'til I tell the guys on the web. I'll be famous.*

He smiles as he listens to the sirens fading in the distance. Evasion and escape, just like he was trained. Ten more minutes, then he'll return to base. *Bravo Zulu, dude. Fucking good job.*

Chapter 6

D*amn.*

The first pass of my facial recognition software comes up negative for the shooter from Barbie's video. I barely register the sun at high noon outside the hotel window.

I open another program, this one for military personnel, and launch the search. While it's working, I check on my computer's alerts, set to grab any notifications for women and children sex trafficking and child sex tourism.

My heart hurts when I recall my recent side hustle work trip to the Dominican Republic, where sex trafficking runs rampant because prostitution is legal. I was with the FBI when they busted a group of scum US citizens on an organized child sex tourism trip. *Talk about taking advantage of the country's youngest victims.* I'm always on the lookout for another similar mission to catch those perv—

The computer dings. Adrenaline swells as I switch screens and find about a hundred possible matches. I let out a breath. I'll need to go through each one manually. I position one window on the left of my screen with a large freeze-frame of the shooter's face from the young woman's video, and on the right, I open the facial recognition possibilities. I had searched through about a dozen when my cell rings. It's the news desk from AODN.

"Banks," I answer bruskly.

"TJ, Albuquerque PD is holding a news conference in an hour," barks the same young female's voice from before. "Need ya to cover it."

"Britt, you know I don't do news conferences. Hire some local yocal. Besides, I might be close to finding the shooter." I click on another image.

"Wait, what? How?"

"Got cell video from a witness. Perp might be former military."

"No shit, good job, TJ," Brittney, the assignment editor, says. "When can we have it?"

"Not 'til I go through it first. Cops don't know I have it yet." I flip to the next photo.

"La, la, la, I didn't hear that."

"Good, so let me get back to work." I tap my earpiece and disconnect the call.

I will eventually turn over the footage. Chances are someone will question why I didn't provide it to the cops sooner. I'll work out a reason, and—

Shit, there he is. I stop on an image and compare it to Barbie's video. I run a few more frames of the digital footage and pause it, looking again.

Quadruple gold.

I snap a photo of the information, grab my phone and camera bag and race out of the hotel room.

Chapter 7

U *don't get greedy. U get in, get out. Those bozos who are caught and shot stay too long.*

In a small motel room, the mid-afternoon sun streaming through the skinny blinds, Patrick finishes the post on his cell phone and sends it to the Skins14 website. He takes a long slug of beer, and as he sets the can down, his eyes momentarily land on his right hand with the SS symbol tattoo. He flexes and grips his fingers, smiling as the pair of lightning bolts—the ancient Germanic letter "S"—representing Hitler's secret police move up and down, as if striking.

Chapter 8

The tall, broad-shouldered man with a thick neck and bulging thighs nearly fills the frame of his FBI workplace door.

"Banks. Whatcha need?"

"Hey, Porter. Can we step inside?" I glance at the receptionist who watches me with a suspicious frown.

FBI Special Agent Aaron Porter steps back and gestures with an ebony hand for me to enter. He closes the door after them.

"Tick-tock, Banks."

"Right. I have something I think you'll be interested in, but I need a deal."

Porter eases his tall frame gracefully into a high-back chair behind his desk. "I'm listening."

"So, I was at the mall shooting, and ran across a woman who was a witness. Turns out she has video of the shooter."

He looks at me with an expression that is hard to read. "And you didn't turn it over to law enforcement immediately because—?"

"Hey, you know me, Porter. I wanted a shot at it first," I respond, unapologetically.

"And—?"

I roll a small black and white tube marked "ChapStick" toward Porter. He frowns, but catches it and pops off the lid, to reveal a flash drive. He raises his eyebrows at me.

I give a little grin and shrug my shoulders as he puts the disguised device into his computer. "He's ex-military. Maybe white supremacist. Don't think he lives around here."

"And why shouldn't I charge you with obstruction?"

I put my palms on the desk and lean over, my face coming within inches of Porter's mahogany skin. "Because we sure didn't have anything obstructing us last March at that Old Town Albuquerque hotel room."

Now it's my turn to raise my eyebrows at him, as I recall the powerful, wild sex we had last time I was on assignment in his city.

"So true." He holds my gaze. "Another round?"

I pause, continuing to stare intently into his dark chocolate brown eyes, inhaling the breath mint from his mouth. "Possibly. Do we have a deal?"

He chuckles. "That's affirmative. But I need the witness's info."

I straighten up, pull out my cell phone and press a button. "All texted to you. And thanks."

I head for the door.

"You told anyone else about this footage?" Porter asks.

I open the door and step into the foyer, not stopping. "Only my news organization."

"Damnit, Banks!"

"Tick-tock, Porter." My voice trails off as I continue toward the elevator.

Chapter 9

Patrick finishes the fourth can of beer and shoots it toward the waste basket like a high three-pointer on the basketball court.

Only it misses and bounces onto the old carpet, remnants of the liquid adding to the many stains already there from years of abuse.

But Patrick could give a shit. He clicks between the eight channels on the old TV in his motel room.

Every station is carrying the mall shooting. From the big network news to the small local ones, his work is everywhere. He opens another can and slugs back a drink every time he hears, "No suspect has been identified," or "The shooter has eluded police," or "The killer is on the run and is considered armed and dangerous."

Patrick smiles. From his fake ID to the burner phone he bought at a discount big box store, he knows he'll never be found.

He takes another swig of beer, and in no big hurry, begins to pack his few belongings.

Chapter 10

I really wanna find that mall shooter while I'm here in Albuquerque.
Always Online Digital News just released the cell phone images from Barbie and the facial recognition software, so his name and face are out there. The FBI also has his basic info, so they should be able to squeeze him out soon.

Back in my hotel room, I search several skinhead websites, alt-right forums and blogs to find any conversations about the massacre. Lots of messages, but I haven't found anyone bragging about their involvement yet. I make up a few usernames and post questions like "Would sure like to meet the righteous dude who did the brave shooting in Albuquerque!" and "Anyone know the brother from the N.M. attack? he should be made prez of the freakin' usa!" But no luck.

Using a bootleg copy of a motor vehicle department software, I find a red 1998 Dodge Charger registered to the perp, Patrick Newberry, from a rural route in Cherry, Arizona. I check a map and the location is way off the grid in the northern mountains of the state.

I also open a new app called RealTimeEYZ, which consists of flying drones that can do certain specific searches. Considered to be too "big brotherly" for city police departments, it is mostly used underground and by a few rogue CIA and FBI agents, which is how I got it.

I have a gut feeling Newberry is still in the area, so I set a 50-mile radius and start the overhead search for the vehicle. I watch it work for a couple of minutes until an alert on another computer window gets my attention. I open the screen from a skinhead web forum and there's a response to my request to contact the Albuquerque shooter. It says: *He's one crazy white mother-fucker at WhitePowerRWSTM.* I recognize the initials to include RWS, or Right Wing Strategic, an influential conservative nationalist group which is run by Ted Miller, a controversial white supremacist who founded the organization in the early 2000s.

I search for the web handle and hit the motherlode when I discover Newberry's rants about Jews, blacks, Muslims—and the shooting. He portrays a certain intelligence, yet with a very narrow-minded view of how the world works.

Beep-beep-beep. Back to the RealTimeEYZ screen, where the program has identified 32 vehicles matching my search criteria. *Yes!* Now I need to go through them individually to figure out which one is Newberry's.

I start nearest the Albuquerque mall. I narrow down the possibilities to about half a dozen local motels, hotels and fast-food restaurants, and determine addresses for them.

I dial a TV production assistant I hired during another recent shoot in town. He's in his early 20s, street-smart and hungry.

"Ross, you working?" I ask.

"Yeah, I'm schleppin' coffee on a car commercial," Ross responds in a low voice. "Whassup?"

"How much they paying you?"

"A hundred a day, why?"

"I'll double that if you can walk off right now and do a job for me. Probably just take you a couple of hours."

"You got it, TJ. Whaddaya want me to do?"

"Find a car."

I text Ross the Charger's license plate number and several addresses in the order I want him to check them out. I take half a dozen more leads and head out in my rental car to do the same.

Chapter 11

Patrick is already planning his next attack.

This time it might be at one of those Jewish temples or synagogues or maybe a mosque, or whatever they call 'em. Maybe even a smaller city this time, so they don't have much security and he can once again sneak in and—

Patrick's burner phone, the one he purchased at a discount big-box store, blows up with bells and other notifications.

Mug of coffee in hand, Patrick was leisurely getting ready to leave Albuquerque in his beloved old Dodge Charger when the urgent tones start. He checks the cell for the source, and finds multiple messages on the same board he posted to earlier. "Dude, yur busted" and "watch out for the cops" are just two of the many posts he sees.

He quickly turns on the TV and sees a grainy shot of his old Army photo, his face half-obscured by a green cap. *Shit.*

Patrick slams the cup onto the dresser and brown liquid splashes out onto the wood surface. He throws the rest of his items into the duffle bag when he hears himself singing at the mall. His heads snaps to the television screen to watch the video. His mouth falls open.

"I love my country, the USA. But I won't give it over to the Jews who betray."

Fuck!

In the shot, he's wearing a different cap that mostly covers his eyes, but the TV puts that image next to the military picture. An announcer reads the news.

"In this exclusive report, Always Online Digital News believes the suspected shooter who killed more than 32 people and injured a dozen more this morning at Albuquerque Fashion Center mall is Patrick Newberry, whose last known address is in northern Arizona. The FBI confirms they also have the information, from an anonymous source, but will not release additional details. If anyone recognizes Newberry, police say not to approach, but to call 911, as the suspect is assumed to be armed and dangerous. Always Online Digital News will keep you informed with further…"

Fucking hell! Patrick hurriedly stuffs the rest of his belongings in his backpack and jams the assault rifle on top.

Chapter 12

I get a text from Ross: *found it*, with the address of a no-tell-motel about five miles from the shooting scene.

I text back: *thx! now get outta there. will send $*

I race to the location, and while enroute, alert my FBI buddy, Aaron Porter, along with local Albuquerque PD.

Two police squad cars, running full lights but no sirens, pull into the parking lot of the motel just ahead of me. I squeal to a stop behind them, grab my camera and start taping.

The officers climb out of their vehicles, weapons drawn. They search around the asphalt lot, but there's no red Dodge Charger.

"Shit. He musta just left," I yell as I sprint toward the cops. "You need to put out a BOLO for the car."

A stocky officer with a buzz cut whips his weapon towards me. "Stop right there."

"Whoa, whoa, hold on." I put my hands up in the air. "Stay cool. I'm media."

Buzz Cut lowers his gun but does not holster it. "You the one who called this in? Who are you? Let's see some ID." The other one, a taller, lean man with balding gray hair cautiously steps about 15 feet around the other side of me.

"Guys, he's getting away. It's the mall shooter. He was just here."

The two men look at each other briefly and Buzz Cut gives a side nod of his head to Gray Hair, who gets on his radio but stays near me.

"I said, ID."

I shake my head, pulling out my press credentials from around my neck. "I'm with Always Online Digital News and covered the shooting this morning. His car was spotted here, so he still must be close. We gotta go!"

Buzz Cut, whose badge reads "M. Worsold," hands back my identification, a scowl on his face. "Howdja know he was here?" His forehead perspires in the warm afternoon sun.

I sigh in exasperation. "I have my ways. Look, we gonna get a move on, or do you wanna be the guy who lets the shooter get away?"

The other officer rushes over. "It's legit. Got FBI confirmation."

"He's from Arizona." I pull up my cell phone's map. "My guess is he's going to jump on the 45 to hit I-40 then go straight west on his way back there. But seriously, his car was here about eight minutes ago, so he can't be far."

The tall man's radio squawks with a female dispatcher's voice. "Suspect vehicle license Charlie David Alpha 7-2-7 heading southbound on Irving Boulevard."

"Let's go." The officers run to their respective vehicles as I race to mine. Buzz Cut calls out, "You! Stay. Do not follow."

I pause with my hand on the driver side door handle. "Copy that," I respond. But as soon as the two squad cars peel out of the motel parking lot, I do the same. "*'Stay.'* Fuck that shit. I'm not a dog," I scoff as I jump in the seat, start the ignition and reach up to turn on my dashboard-mounted camera.

By now, there are two black SUVs, probably FBI, plus five Albuquerque squad cars, a police helicopter and my rental in hot pursuit of the suspected mall shooter Patrick Newberry.

Other civilian vehicles on Irving Boulevard dutifully pull over as the law enforcement squadron runs full Code 3 lights and sirens. My excitement mounting, I stay on their tail, my dash cam capturing the action.

My scanner app, tuned to Albuquerque Police Department, updates me. "Suspect vehicle approaching I-45."

"Fox 140, I've got eyes on suspect vehicle, approaching Eagle Ranch Road."

"Roger, Fox 140."

"Chopper 2, we are approaching suspect vehicle."

"Roger, Chopper 2."

Chapter 13

Patrick's rear-view mirror is filled with flashing cop car lights.

"Go, go, go…" Sweat drips into his eyes, and he swipes his forehead with the arm of his shirt.

Almost at I-45. Both hands tightly gripping the steering wheel of his Charger, he swerves in and out of street traffic, loving the thrill of his beauty's supremacy underneath him. He reaches the freeway and forces the accelerator farther towards the floor. The car leaps with additional power and for a moment, he smiles as he puts significant space between himself and his pursuers as he goes up the ramp and onto the expressway.

But the smile is short-lived when he hears the *thup-thup-thup* of helicopter rotary blades above him.

"Oh fuck, oh fuck, oh fuck." Patrick's heart is nearly exploding in his chest. *This can't be happening. It was going so well. I shoulda split Albuquerque sooner. What the fuck am I gonna to do? I can't just give up, goddamnit. No, but I'll go out in a blaze of glory for the cause if I have to. Yeah, that's what I'll do, I'll—*

He's interrupted by a voice overhead. "Patrick Newberry, this is Albuquerque Police. Pull your vehicle over to the right immediately."

"Like hell!" Patrick pushes his right foot all the way down, and his car, his buddy, his companion, surges forward even faster. "Yes!" Patrick shouts, noting his faithful ride will be due for an oil change when they arrive home.

He whips back and forth across the white lines, barely missing a couple of other cars, and ends up on the far-left shoulder, where he races ahead without anyone in front of him.

Chapter 14

It's times like these I'm glad I nabbed the only Chevy Camaro SS on the rental lot, as its 426 horsepower V8 easily keeps up with the cop cars and the fugitive.

My portable scanner app crackles with updates.

"Chopper 2, we're right above suspect vehicle. Fox 140, can you push him off on exit 38A?"

"Fox 140, he's traveling about 100 miles an hour, lane five, concerned about vehicular traffic on the freeway."

The dispatcher's voice comes on. "All units, traffic break at milepost 455. All units, I-45 is blocked at exit 460 with Stop Sticks. Repeat, traffic break at milepost 455 and I-45 is blocked at exit 460 with Stop Sticks."

The chase will come to an end in a few minutes as soon as Patrick's car hits the traffic spikes and they blow out all his tires. The police and FBI vehicles follow a distance behind him in the three left lanes, so I pull my gun-metal gray Camaro over one lane to the right to see if I can spot Patrick. The red Charger is flying along the freeway and nearly hits another car that hasn't fully pulled over.

"Move, damnit!" I yell as I continue my pursuit. *Milepost 452. Not long now.*

Chapter 15

Patrick is surprised when no other cars are on the freeway beside or in front of him, only those chasing him from behind.

It takes a couple of seconds to register, and then flashing lights catch his attention: a bunch of cop cars parked right on the freeway, dead ahead.

Goddamnit! Think, think, thi—

His eyes glimpse a long, narrow, red-and-white something in the lane in front of him, but the words "Stop Sticks" aren't readable until the second before he runs over it and his tires explode with a huge boom, boom. It's all Patrick can do to keep his car under control as he slams on the brakes and skids to a halt, inches from two police squad cars. Immediately half a dozen rifles and guns point straight at him from behind the cop cars.

Chapter 16

I continue to follow Buzz Cut's squad car behind the Department of Public Safety vehicle's zigzagging traffic break to slow westbound vehicles.

I'll probably be ticketed for it later. *Won't be the first time.* Whichever news organization I'm working for usually either pays the fine or makes a contribution to the law enforcement body in question, so the ticket goes away. They're after the same thing I am: the first footage.

Brake lights ahead. White smoke in the air. Stop Sticks have done their job. I press Record on my hand-held video unit, then maneuver my car to the far right of the freeway so my dashcam will continue to videotape a wide shot of the entire scene. I stop the car, jump out and run toward the thinning chemical clouds and flashing cop car lights.

Chapter 17

Through the smoke, Patrick hears, "Hands on the steering wheel! Now!"

He instinctively obeys, but thinks about the next steps. *If I stay here, I'm a sitting duck and will go to prison like, forever. Not my style. No way.*

The white clouds dissipating, Patrick calmly reaches for his AR-15 and slides another magazine into the weapon. He eases his car door open. *Now or never. Blaze of glory. The Skins14 boys will be talking about me for years.*

"Remain in the vehicle! Do not move!" yells another stern voice.

With the rifle in his right hand, Patrick points it towards the cops and makes a run for it, off to the side of the freeway. *Blaze of glory! Blaze of glory!*

Multiple gunshots blast through the air. Some zing by his ear, others cause amazingly little pain. He doesn't even feel his legs go out from under him, but is surprised to feel the warm, rough asphalt under his left cheek. *Blaze of...*and then nothing.

Chapter 18

Death by cop is not pretty.

But it makes for amazing footage. And at the primo late afternoon "golden hour" to boot.

It couldn't have been choreographed better if it had been a movie. The almost-setting sun creates the beautiful deep buttery glow that only comes for a few minutes once a day.

I have Patrick in my viewfinder and follow him getting out of the car, gun pointed at the cops, starting to run. I widen the shot to include the more than half a dozen officers beside their vehicles with weapons drawn, then shooting, creating their own gun smoke. I'm determined to keep the camera stabilized, steady, even throughout the multiple blasts. The *boom, boom, pop, boom, pop, pop* continues for what seems like a minute but is only about 10 seconds, according to the camera's runtime monitor. Then silence, and Newberry is on the ground, blood slowly encircling him.

The officers cautiously lower their guns and someone says "Hold fire." I find the voice's form with my viewfinder and continue to roll as he creeps carefully toward the downed man. He's short, stocky, with an earpiece cord spiraling down to a clip on his crisp white shirt, no dark jacket. Shoulder holster strapped to his body. Handgun, Glock, pointed at Newberry. He reaches his left hand towards the suspect's throat. His right weapon hand relaxes as he straightens up, left hand fingers in the air signaling "come." Other officers walk toward the bo—

"What the fuck are you doing here?" Buzz Cut shouts from behind me.

Uh-oh. I whip my camera around and continue to videotape the red-faced officer who instructed me to obey like a damned animal. *What was his name?* "Officer Worsold, congratulations on taking down the suspect. This must be a good moment for you and your law enforcement colleagues." I keep the camera at my eye, zooming in on my subject.

"Wha—? You—I mean…" Worsold stammers. Then recovers, puffs up his chest. "Well, of course, it was a joint effort by Albuquerque PD, the FBI, DPS. We—" Worsold stops. "Wait a fuckin' minute. Stop your camera, now!"

"Sir, this is public property, and I have First Amendment rights to be here and to show exactly how local law enforcement took down this murderer to protect the community. Thanks for all your efforts." With that, I walk swiftly toward the Hold Fire guy, hoping for a statement, leaving Buzz Cut with his mouth open, eyes blinking rapidly.

It's not quite 8 p.m., and I'm done editing the last of the video footage.

I send it off to the newsroom, pleased with the images and natural sound I shot. Even more pleased with the executive producer's promise of a sizable bump in my next paycheck.

I take a long, hot shower, and once again "style" my short, wet hair with one hand, spiking the ends up and around my face.

From my suitcase, I unroll a little black dress. As I slip it on, a quick glance at the mirror keeps check on a flat stomach, lean frame, muscled arms and legs. *Not bad for almost 40.* I slide into a pair of black, flat ballet shoes, satisfied with how well both items travel in my bag and ease out for this occasion. *A special occasion for a job well done.*

I carefully apply blood red lipstick, put the lid back on and toss it inside a small black crossover evening bag. I head out into the night.

Two glasses of Chivas on the rocks later, I survey the dance club with its pounding music, flashing lights and gyrating bodies.

I linger on a tall, muscular man in khaki pants and a light blue polo shirt, his rich bronze face in stark contrast. He leans back against the bar, drinking from a short glass. My stomach gets a warm, tingly feeling. The man's eyes, also in search mode, connect with mine and we observe each other for a few moments.

I make my way around the dance floor to Blue Polo. "How's it goin'?" I ask in a voice too quiet to be heard above the din. When Blue Polo puts his head closer to mine and asks, "Say again?" I plant an urgent

French kiss on the man's mouth, and my taste buds explode with the flavor of strong cinnamon mint mixed with whiskey when my tongue merges with his. I whisper, "Let's get outta here."

FBI Agent Aaron Porter throws back the remainder of his drink and lets me lead him out by the hand.

Chapter 19

Darkmover saunters among the men and women sitting at laptop computers behind dozens of tables, eyeing their work, one eyebrow raised.

The calm, murmuring conversations are in a variety of foreign tongues.

Larger monitors on the wall connect to the computers, black cables snaking around in every direction. Small portable servers sit under each table, green lights blinking. Large aluminum cases on wheels line one wall, ready for a quick exit.

If needed.

Hands loosely clasped in back, Darkmover surveys the activity of hackers, cyber whizzes and others willing to do the bidding of one of the most—no, *the* most powerful sex trafficker in the world.

Business is good.

Chapter 20

Back in my hotel room, I'm antsy.

No immediate assignments on the horizon, I go back to my second "mission:" to scour my usual Internet contacts in the women sex trafficking world for a story to dive into. But at the slow rate law enforcement works, nothing is ready for a video camera to expose them.

I grab my jump rope, one of the few things I always carry with me, and begin my 40 fast single reps. Great cardio, excellent overall workout for legs and arms, easy to take everywhere. It also helps me think.

Aaron's words haunt me from last night. *Time to settle down, Banks. Enjoy your life. Quit living for the next big story.*

I'll admit to being jealous of his beautiful Pueblo-style adobe home in Albuquerque. Thick magenta bougainvillea on trellises surround the perimeter, and rust-colored pavers lead to the arched gate outside the massive wooden front door. Gleaming terracotta floors, bookshelves filled with his collection of reading materials, beautiful bedroom suite of matching Southwest furniture.

Next 40 reps. Add crisscross.

Is that it? Do I need a place of my own? My military parents moved around so much during my upbringing, "putting down roots" wasn't a thing. Until they retired, and are now living in Florida, where my meager belongings are stored in their guestroom closet.

And when was the last time I saw or even talked to them? I'm embarrassed to think about it. Same with the few friends I have scattered around the world. Lizbeth. Katrina. Roger. Sure, I talk to Roger for work, but with the brief exception of yesterday morning, it's not like the old days when he and I would talk for hours.

Then there were Aaron's last words as I left early this morning. "How about calling when you don't *need* something?" Like a deal. Or sex. The words are burned in my brain.

Another 40 reps done, I put my hands on my knees while my breath slows and my heart returns to normal.

Growing up, I spent a lot of time by myself. My parents were always working. Mom would be deployed to another JAG post in another country, and I'd stay with Dad until he was sent on another military intelligence mission, and then I'd live with Mom. Rinse and repeat.

Who cares? Enough introspection.

It's *my* life, *my* terms, *my* rules.

I toss the jump rope on the bed.

Back to work.

A brief conversation with the front desk, and I can extend my current hotel stay for at least another two weeks.

As good a place as any. Great restaurants within walking distance, decent view of the 10-thousand foot Sandia Mountains, strong coffee. *And Aaron Porter?*

Can't let him cloud my decision. Sure, so maybe he was part of the reason for me telling Roger Lester to keep me out of his assignment rotation for the next month, prolonging it from the original "few days." Roger isn't happy about that. He gets a cut from the gigs he assigns me, although he swears that is not the reason.

"I just want you to be safe, TJ," he tells me.

Yeah, well, if it was safety I was after, I'd be sitting on a rocking chair in a house behind a white picket fence. *Not my style.*

I wasn't able to tell him and still can't completely justify why I made the decision to go on hiatus from crime news to focus solely on exposing women sex traffickers for at least the next few weeks. Everyone knows it's a horrible crime, one that forces millions of people across the globe into the dangerous and often deadly world of human trafficking. More than half are women and children, and a quarter are bought and sold as sex slaves.

Maybe it's partly because of a close friendship with a girl, Katrina, in my Bitburg Air Force Base High School in Germany. The Greek daughter of another JAG attorney, we did homework together, giggled about boys and were a constant duo. We shared secrets with each other we would never breathe to another person.

She'd take me shopping, something I never liked much. She looked adorable in those frilly dresses, with her petite figure, olive skin and long dark hair, where I'd just look like a dork.

But she was restless, always seeking out new adventures.

I think I learned to take risks from her. Like the time we snuck out of our base housing while our parents were at the Officer's Club. She sweet-talked a young MP into letting us pass through the guard gate, even though it was after curfew. We dashed to the closest bar just outside the gates and managed to get a couple of drunk soldiers to buy us a drink. We made it back before anyone noticed and were so proud of that escapade.

Then there was the day we "borrowed" my dad's Jeep, drove 100 miles across the border to Belgium and bought a bottle of their Dutch gin, Jenever. Of course, we started drinking it on the way back and were totally looped by the time we returned. We were both grounded for a couple of weeks, but we laughed and laughed about how crazy we were to do that.

Our senior year, when she told me she'd met a man who was going to take her traveling with him, she jumped at the chance, despite my warning that he was too old for her and had "con man" written all over his face.

She said she was in love, and they left.

I'd receive occasional postcards at first, from different countries, and I always sensed despair and regret in her few words. But with no return address, and later with my roving lifestyle, I lost touch.

Typical trafficker. He was grooming her, controlling her and isolating her from friends and family to lead her into a sex ring. I vowed to eventually find out, and I'm always on the lookout for a picture of her beautiful face.

But the investigations I've worked on were small, barely skimming the surface of the operations generating an estimated $99 billion annually. I want to help nab the big kingpins, the scum who were making millions off the backs of these women.

That's where the deep web and the darknet come in.

Chapter 21

Gotta find Cho.

I search my contacts for the young Asian woman I worked with during a Thailand exposé of a sex trafficking ring a couple of years ago. Her technology skills were crazy brilliant, and while I knew a little about the deep web, she was the first to tell me about the darknet.

"Darknet not illegal," she told me then, and I expressed my surprise at that. "It often used to shield classified government activity. Human rights activists also protected on darknet by oppressive foreign regimes. Journalists, too, can use."

At that time, it was my first foray into the seedy underworld of many illegal trades: pornography, drugs, weapons, sadism, torture, even murder. And of course, the sex trafficking of women and children.

Another cyber security expert told me there are many more sex trafficking organizations on the regular Internet we use every day. She said it was in the billions, compared to maybe 20-thousand sites on the deep web. Her explanation of those shopping their wares on the deep web: "They're just more paranoid."

Regardless, regular search engines can't access the deep web pages and so are hidden, accessed only by passwords and specific authorizations. It's become a fully functional marketplace for hidden criminal activity.

My research shows the darknet is more purposefully hidden, meaning it's designed for anonymity. Unlike the surface web and dark web, the darknet is only accessible with special tools and software. And because identities are anonymous and untraceable, illegal activities like human trafficking or drug dealing take place unchecked on the darknet.

Cho's name and contact info in Los Angeles pop up in my phone's contacts. I text her a quick note to call me.

I figure it might be awhile before she gets back to me, so I start a rep with my jump rope. My cell rings. Caller ID says CHO CYBER GEEK. I toss down the rope and click Answer. "Hey, Cho, thanks for calling back so fast. How are you?"

"Good to hear from you, TJ. I am fine. Where you be past three years?"

Ouch, has it been that long? "Oh, you know me. Covering anything that bleeds." *What a sad but true description.* "So, Cho, you remember telling me about the darknet back then? Are you still investigating trafficking there?"

"Oh, yes." Cho's voice reflects a bit of resignation. "Still plenty sharks in that ocean."

"I'm taking a break from news and would like to go after some of those bigger sharks. Large operations. Not the smaller pimps. Can you help me find them?"

"Who you work for?" she asks. "You have budget?"

Good questions. And Cho is always the savvy businesswoman. Usually, it's a news or governmental organization that hires and bankrolls me, my travel, hiring people like Cho and allowing us access into an operation.

"It's actually not an assignment… yet," I explain. "And I have funds I've saved. I'll take care of you."

"I not worried about me. Darknet dangerous. You need protection."

Chapter 22

P*rotection?!*

"You need FBI, CIA," Cho says.

Ahh. She's probably right. I can't just burst into the darknet by myself and expect to single-handedly capture some giant kingpins.

"Or middleman," she offers.

"Is that you?"

"Oh, no," she chuckles. "But I can probably find."

"Great. Are you seeing any particular movement recently?"

Cho pauses. "I know you like go after women and girls sex trafficking, yes? But there is something else you should look into."

Slightly disappointed, I shake my head. *I don't want to be distracted from my primary mission.* "I don't know, Cho. I'm kinda focused on those victims."

"Has to do with trafficking migrant children."

My adrenaline spikes. "Really? Whatcha got?"

"Not on regular phone line, TJ. Prefer talk on PGP line."

"Oh yeah, 'pretty good privacy' with encryption, right?"

"Yes. Let me gather intel and I send you link."

"Thanks, Cho. It will be good to work with you again."

We hang up. My heart is racing as I wonder what she has discovered. Then I hear Roger's voice: "I just want you to be safe, TJ."

I grab the jump rope and start twirling, fast.

Hell, I don't plan to put myself in danger. But the minute it comes out of my mouth, I realize no one does, and yet I manage to get myself in plenty of trouble, like the highspeed chase of Patrick Newberry the other day.

But depending on what I find out from Cho, I could contact Aaron and see if the FBI will be my front. Maybe they're already on it.

Aaron. *Time to settle down, TJ,* he'd said.

Is it? How many more assignments, how many more years can I keep doing this? Is there something else I want to do? Nothing immediately comes to the mind of this adrenaline-fueled news junkie.

After three reps of 40 with the rope, I'm breathing hard and sweat drips down my face. I lean over, catch my breath, and see stains on the carpet. *Yuck.* I gaze around the room, my "home" for the next seven to 14 days. *Blah. Uninspiring. Gross with other people's shit.*

Maybe I could get a little studio apartment in a big city, near the airport, where I could call home base. I could get some furniture, and...

What the hell am I thinking? I'm not a decorator, have never lived anywhere longer than a year or two, other than a college dorm or a short-term furnished rental during my early career days. Never spent much time there, as it was mostly a place to crash. Now it's usually no more than a week in the same hotel.

But I admit it was nice to sleep in "my" bed. Have my clothes hung in a closet rather than always stuffed in a suitcase. Maybe I could eventually get a cat...

Oh, for god's sake, don't be ridiculous. You'll still never be there long enough to take care of an animal.

I decide to take a shower and put those thoughts out of my head. For now.

Chapter 23

a blinking blue light above one computer monitor in the war room gets Darkmover's attention.

A smile at the thought of the "blue light special" at a now defunct discount big box store in the United States of America.

"Yes?" Darkmover asks, standing next to the operator in front of his laptop.

"*SIN42 dobbiamo muoverci in fretta*," states the young man with long hair.

"Een English, Antonio," Darkmover urges.

"SIN42 need to move fast. Getting some heat."

Darkmover surveys a massive roll-up screen on the wall. A finger touch brings up all the sites in the India jurisdiction.

"Hmm… new home, new adventures." Darkmover points on the map. "To Punjab."

Chapter 24

Clean, energized and dressed in my trademark black jeans, black T-shirt and black boots, I open the link Cho sent through pgptool.org.

She explained it's a secure online way to communicate with encryption so no one else can read it. I download the private key she sent and type:

TJ: *Can you chat?*

A few seconds later, her message appears.

Cho: *Yes. Am tracking situation that may have broad reach across US, probably Mexico, maybe Europe, dealing with migrant children separated from families at the border.*

I use my microphone:

T: *What about them? Many have still not been reunited with their parents.*

C: *Turns out some supposed foster homes are really sex and human trafficking sites.*

What?! How can that be? I thought the kids were supposed to be placed with families until the parents went through the court system and could get their young ones back.

T: *Unbelievable! Who's working it? Homeland Security?*

C: *Yes, and DHHS.*

Department of Health and Human Services. I type in a quick regular Internet search for "migrant children trafficked" and a couple of small news stories pop up, including one from Ohio where at least six children were lured to the U.S. from Guatemala with the promise of a better life, but were forced to work on egg farms and live in squalor. Another group of 15 kids from Honduras were sent to a "foster home" in upstate New York where pornographic photos were shot and distributed, and all the boys and girls, ranging in age from 8 to 17, were forced into prostitution.

T: *Got someone I can talk to?*

Cho texts two names, phone numbers and email addresses from her contacts. One is Kate O'Brien from DHHS, the other is Cooper Miller from Homeland Security. I save the contacts.

T: *Let me get briefed. U watching some websites?*

C: *Yes. Reg, deep web, darknet.*

T: *Got it. Thx. U still live in LA?*

C: *Yes*

T: *Need refresher course in darknet safety.*

C: *U come stay here again. I show u.*

She sends me her address, the same condo overlooking Venice Beach where I spent a few days during that Thailand investigation. I recall a very tiny but neat and clean one-bedroom close to a fabulous Chinese restaurant. The thought of their spicy squid makes my mouth water.

Her living room is her office, filled with computers, monitors, hard drives, scanners, everything a cyber investigator would need. She rarely leaves her place, except to eat.

T: *TY, u rock! Will let u know ETA. BFN*

C: *Bye*

I sign out of the PGP site. I look around the hotel room again and realize I won't be staying another two weeks after all. *See? No point getting a place of my own. I'd never stick around.* I call the front desk to notify them of my new plans.

Chapter 25

Seated at the hotel room's small desk with my phone set to record, I brace myself with a cup of strong, hot coffee. I make the first call to Cooper Miller at Homeland Security.

"Miller," a gruff voice answers.

"Mr. Miller, this is TJ Banks. I'm a reporter working on the story of migrant children being sex trafficked. What can you tell me about it?"

"Call PIO," he growls.

"Now, Mr. Cooper, we're both aware that the public information officer is just going to call you, then she'll call me and refer me to you, and we'll be back at this same spot. So, can we just cut to the chase? What is Homeland Security doing to stop this?"

He pauses for a beat. "No comment." Click. Miller hangs up.

That went well. I take a sip of coffee and call DHHS. An administrative assistant answers.

"Yes, may I speak to Kate O'Brien? This is TJ Banks. I'm a reporter working a story that Ms. O'Brien is familiar with."

The gatekeeper lets me right through.

"This is Kate O'Brien."

"Hi, Ms. O'Brien, this is TJ Banks. I'm a reporter and I understand you have knowledge of a situation where migrant children separated from their families at the border are being sex trafficked. I'd like to help you bring these traffickers to justice. What information do you have?"

O'Brien doesn't answer right away. "It's… under investigation," she says finally.

"And?"

Another pause. "And we have not yet released our findings."

"But how could this happen?" I ask. "You're supposed to be protecting these kids."

"We did our best given the impossible position we were in when the zero-tolerance edict came down very quickly and from on high. I'm not making excuses, but we did not have time to put in place the proper protocols, do the appropriate vetting, conduct background checks of all caregivers. And under the current administration, we are being rushed to move the children quickly out of shelters and release them to adults."

"So how did you find out about these kids being trafficked?"

Another pause. "I cannot reveal that, as it's still under investigation."

"How many total cases of sex trafficking and human trafficking have you found?"

"That's still under—"

"Yeah, I get it, under investigation. I'll follow up in another week or so after I speak with my FBI contact and perhaps you can release more information then." We hang up.

Stonewalled. Not unexpected. Happens a lot, especially with government officials.

I dial Aaron Porter's office number. He answers on the second ring.

"Whatcha need, Banks?"

All business today. And there's that dig again about only calling when I need something. I guess it's true, but I ignore it. "Got a lead on sex trafficking of migrant children. The ones separated from their families at the border?"

"Yeah, and?"

"How does that even happen?"

He pauses. "Who are you working for?"

"Well, this isn't an official assignment yet, but if it pans out, I'll pitch it around. Checking to see if the Bureau is already on this."

"Got any contacts?"

I give him the names Cho sent me. "I've already talked to them. Didn't get a lot of information. But they didn't deny it."

"Let me do some checking, Banks."

"Thanks, Porter." *Should I tell him I'm leaving for Los Angeles? Does he really give a damn?*

"Anything else, Banks?"

"Uh, yeah, I'm heading to LA. Getting updated in the latest on deep web and darknet. Got time for a drink tonight before I leave?"

"Damnit, Banks, you shouldn't mess around with that shit."

"Aww, didn't know you cared, Porter."

His frustration is obvious in his heavy sigh. "Be serious, Banks. That's some risky stuff. You could get yourself into something you can't get out of. There are some incredibly dangerous criminals lurking there."

"I'll be careful. I'm working with a top cyber investigator, and she knows her stuff. Wouldn't you like to take down another one of these big organizations, like you did when you seized deepdotweb.com?"

"That's just it. You need to leave the takedowns to us."

"Exactly. I'll just tag along to tell the world about your successful mission."

A scoff from the other end of the phone.

"C'mon, Porter, let's talk more about it later. How about that rooftop restaurant in Old Town, say, 5:30? I know you love their stuffed peppers."

Aaron sighs again, this time as if in resignation. "All right. Meet you there." He clicks off.

Chapter 26

Level 5 restaurant at the Hotel Chaco in Old Town has a nearly 360-degree view of the Sandia Mountains that overlooks the downtown area of Albuquerque on one side and residential homes on the other.

I wait in a comfy stuffed chair next to thick art glass that surrounds the eatery. In front of me is a combination table and firepit, its flames dancing in the reflection of the glass. Lights are twinkling below as the sun sets on my last day in this town, for a while anyway. My bag is packed, I've checked out of the hotel and will catch a 9:30 flight to LAX tonight.

So many things are going through my head. Do I really think I can stay out of breaking news for a month? News addict that I am, it's going to be tough. Will focusing on a meaty sex-trafficking story be enough?

And both Cho and Aaron have warned me about the dangers of the deep web. I was always nervous about using my computer to search there until Cho showed me ways to get in with sites like Signal and Tor. She assured me they offered end-to-end encryption for my journalistic and personal security.

Then came along Qubes, a free and open-source operating system for personal computers that provides security by compartmentalizing and isolating digital files.

Even better, she says, is Authentic8's Silo, which promises isolation from malware and prying eyes on surface, deep and dark websites.

I'll wait to do any more internet research until I see Cho. Or better yet, maybe I'll just hire her as my dark web go-to gal. *Yeah, then I'll stay safe, right?*

But at some point, I've got to get my camera out and catch these scumbags in action.

That can get dicey, and a Kevlar vest with PRESS on the back doesn't guarantee something bad won't happen. Increasingly, news crews have been attacked while working, such as the CNN reporter who was arrested during a Black Lives Matter protest, or the Minneapolis journalist shot by a rubber bullet by police. Or worse, with other journalists being murdered in other countries.

Funny, I never used to consider the danger until recently. *Is that part of getting older? Same with the issue of settling down? Getting that pang of envy when I think of Aaron's house and Cho's apartment? Wondering what it would be like to—*

"Earth to TJ?"

Chapter 27

I look up with a start.

Aaron stands above me, hands on hips, an amused grin on his face.

Wow, he is gorgeous. That beautiful ebony skin. Strong jaw. Soft lips. How tender they felt on mine the other night.

His white shirt is rolled up at the sleeves, which reveals a black tribal tattoo around his forearm. No tie, so just a bit of his muscular chest is exposed through the two open buttons.

"Oh, sorry. Didn't see you come in." *How do I greet someone I've worked with and slept with? Do I stand up? Give him a hug? Shake his hand?*

Aaron solves my quandary by taking a seat in the chair across from me. "You were a few million miles away."

I take a sip of Scotch. "You've given me a lot to think about with those little sermons of yours." I put my finger up to catch the server's eye.

Aaron's eyebrows raise. "Oh, now you think I'm preaching to you?"

Before I can answer, a young man approaches the table. "What can I get you, sir?" he asks Aaron.

"Whiskey, neat."

"And you, ma'am? Would you like another Scotch?"

"Sure, I'm Ubering tonight. And you can put in that appetizer order, please."

"Yes, ma'am." The waiter nods and leaves.

"Ugh, 'ma'am.' Do I look that old?"

"No. You don't," Aaron says emphatically. "You look… amazing." The last word comes out soft, gentle. He looks like he wants to reach for my hands.

There's an awkward pause as I look down at my casual jeans and customary dark T-shirt. No little black dress tonight. "Thanks." *Sheesh, am I embarrassed? What the…*

'So, what was going on in your head when I arrived? Anything you'd like to share?"

"Oh, maybe… all that talk about 'enjoying life, stop chasing the next big story, time to settle down…'"

"Huh. You actually listened to me. Whaddaya know."

Chapter 28

The server comes back with our drinks and the stuffed peppers and sets them down.

The warmth of the fire pit feels good on my arms. I stare at the flames flickering among the glass globs, crackling lightly. The heavenly smell of the spices makes my mouth salivate.

Aaron takes a slow sip of his drink. "How long have we known each other, TJ? Four, five years now? Yet last night was the first time we've had a significant, personal kind of conversation."

I keep looking at the fire. I don't dare glance into those dark brown eyes of his. "True. I just…" I don't go any further.

"At the risk of sounding preachy, you know it's okay to trust people once in a while. And when it works both ways, that's pretty cool." He takes a bite of stuffed pepper and catches a drip of sauce on his napkin.

Uh-oh. Sounding mighty similar to the "let others in" thing Roger said. I look at him now. "What, you think I don't trust you? Are you kidding? All the times we've worked togeth—"

"I don't mean on the job. I'm talking about like last night. Like now. I'm talking about opening up. Trusting yourself enough to lower that steel door of yours to trust someone else to come a little closer. Like me."

"What do you mean, steel door?" Rhetorical question. It's my barrier of protection, like a damned sci-fi forcefield that I make sure is in place around me 24/7. Protecting…

"What are you so afraid of?" His voice is concerned, like he really wants to know.

I guess that makes two of us. But now this is making me really uncomfortable. I gotta get outta here.

"If I knew the answer, we wouldn't be having this conversation," I say flippantly. "Look, I just wanted to tell you I'm off the breaking-news cycle for now, and I'll be in Los Angeles working on this migrant sex-trafficking story. I promise to be careful and won't get in over my head. I hope if you find out anything, you'll keep me in the loop, and I'll do the same."

Aaron smiles and shakes his head. "I guess that'll have to do for now." He takes a long pull of his whiskey and attacks another pepper.

I finish my second drink. *I'm so not good at this stuff. Why can't I just have an honest conversation with the man? Am I afraid? No. Terrified. Of exposing myself to hurt and heartache. Just like…*

"Look. I'm a Taurus, the bull. I'm stubborn as hell but I'm also dedicated, and I work really hard. I've never been good at trusting people, like you say. I realize I've got to make some major decisions soon, some that might change a lot about what I do and who I am." I pause to look at Aaron's face. "When I… *if* I come up with some answers… you'll be the first to know."

"I can live with that," he says simply. "Just please, don't do anything reckless. Keep me posted on your progress."

"I will, I promise. I… gotta catch my flight." I toss a couple of 20s on the table, reach for my bag and stand up. Aaron is in mid-bite and seems surprised I'm leaving so soon.

"But you haven't eaten any—"

"It's okay. Enjoy 'em. I'll be in touch." I bend to give Aaron a quick peck on the cheek and hustle out.

Chapter 29

Aaron Porter watches TJ walk briskly out the restaurant door, bag over her shoulder.

He shakes his head at her quick exit, but admires her lean, sinewy body, and recalls those powerful long legs wrapped around his waist last night.

He pulls at his whiskey, smooth, warm. The firepit flames are mesmerizing, and he absent-mindedly watches them flicker.

That woman can be so… exasperating. Exhilarating, too, but damned confounding. We were having a real conversation last night, and started again tonight, but… she puts up that barrier and runs the opposite direction.

Did she have some terrible relationship? Bad break-up? Haven't we all?

He thinks back to Sarah, a CPA at a local Albuquerque firm, whom he dated for a couple of years. He thought maybe he came on too strong, pushed too hard, because suddenly she didn't want to be with him anymore. But she said it was her, not him, and he believed her. *Maybe I shouldn't have.*

Did I come on too strong with TJ? No, I think I've been pretty damned patient. Of course, caution also weighs heavily on his mind, as his Bureau colleagues would disapprove of him associating with a member of the media.

His mind goes back to the migrant sex-trafficking intel he found after speaking with TJ at the office this afternoon. There were dozens of cells the FBI, Homeland Security, DHHS, Border Patrol, ICE and Department of Justice had been trying to infiltrate for the past decade. But every time they got close, one site would simply shut down, presumably to open elsewhere. And tracking was next to impossible, given all the encryption tools available.

It all started when the detention centers couldn't keep up with the influx of children pouring across the southern border, and HHS began giving custody of the children to family members or sponsors who were supposed to help them while their immigration cases were reviewed. If the children didn't have relatives in the United States, they were placed in a system that was supposed to resemble foster care.

With the gray areas of the current immigration policy, the tremendous increase in the number of immigrants and the cartels taking control of some areas of the border, it's little wonder some of those kids fell into the wrong hands.

This will be a tricky mission, as he had also heard rumblings of possible internal government corruption involved. And without a direct connection to his Albuquerque office, he wouldn't normally be tapped to investigate.

The FBI doesn't typically get involved in immigration and border issues, but when talking about "children of a tender age," Aaron is reasonably certain this would fit under the Bureau's Child Exploitation and Human Trafficking Task Force. With his intel, he could ask for a temporary transfer.

Because, thinking about TJ going after it on her own, or even with other agents…

Oh, so now you're trying to be her knight in shining armor, Porter? That's a laugh. Like TJ needs someone to rescue her.

Then not to rescue. To help uncover the truth. Protect the American people and uphold the Constitution of the United States.

"Fidelity, Bravery and Integrity."

Aaron finishes off the remaining stuffed pepper, takes the last gulp of his drink and pops a mint into his mouth. He stands to survey the glittering lights below then heads out.

Chapter 30

I t's about 11 p.m. by the time I secure a rental car and drive to Cho's condo overlooking the Venice Beach boardwalk.

The evening is balmy, and while I can hear the ocean waves as I park, it's too dark to see the rolling surf. Tomorrow I'll walk to the beach.

As I drag my rolling suitcase over the smooth concrete sidewalk, in my mind's eye I can see Cho sitting at her computers in her fancy chair, as the girl never really sleeps. She takes light catnaps when needed but will awake when her computer alerts and notifications signal an update or important message.

I walk up to the second floor, find her end unit and ring the doorbell.

A series of clicks and mechanical whirrings sound as the multiple locks on her door open.

"Hi, Cho."

"Come in, TJ." She gives me a brief hug then closes and secures the door again. "Put your things in bedroom. All ready for you."

"Seriously, I can sleep on the sofa, Cho, I don't want to—"

"No worry. I don't use bedroom anymore. Just sleep here, remember?"

She gestures to her space-age gaming chair in red and black leather, which fits in with the décor, also mostly red and black Oriental fabrics, wall hangings and other knick-knacks.

It looks like she's gained a little weight since I saw her last, but it's hard to tell under her loose kimono in pink and white silk. She's short, barely five feet tall, and like before, probably still doesn't get much exercise. Her long blue-black hair is parted in the middle and streams down her back.

"Thanks. I'll be right back." I take my bag to the room off the living area, use the bathroom, and when I come back, she's engulfed in her huge chair. There's a large aluminum beverage container in the armchair cupholder—probably her usual black tea—and she's monitoring her computer screens.

"You hungry? I call for Chinese if you want." She remembers how much I like the restaurant down the street.

"I'm good, but for sure tomorrow. Unless you want something."

She shakes her head, and her face becomes somber. "You really want tackle this beast?" Her dark eyes are very serious.

"You put it that way, yes, even more so."

"Lots of bad people in trafficking, you know. Even worse, maybe bad people in U.S. government, too."

"Wait. You think there's inside government corruption as well?" I get goosebumps on my arms.

She shrugs. "Maybe. Not found yet. But likely."

I ponder that. *Of course. How else would the kids be sent to traffickers if there wasn't someone on the inside?* "Sounds like you're trying to talk me out of it, like a few others I know." I consider Roger's "I want you to be safe," and Aaron's "Don't do anything reckless."

"No. Just go in with, how you say, 'eyes wide open.'"

I've rarely been one to hesitate, usually jumping into whatever fray is next. But even she's making me nervous.

"What are you saying, Cho?"

"Normal situation, good guys versus bad guys. This time, may not be able to tell who good guys are."

"You mean, those who would normally be the good guys, in our government, may be working both sides. Hard to ferret out."

She nods. "I keep you safe on computer. But you go in with camera, you need more protection."

I see where she's going. I'm usually on the "right" side, the news seeking the truth, exposing evil alongside a law enforcement agency. If I don't have an official assignment with the safety and security a large cable or online outfit affords, it's just me, on my own. I wipe my sweaty hands on my jeans. And it's going to be more complex, assuming there may be a wildcard corrupt official out there. *Can I do this on my own? Do I need to wait until I can find more help?* That also means more foot-dragging, and the investigation will take longer.

Fatigue hits me like a stone wall. I squeeze my eyes shut.

"Look, Cho, I'm beat. It's been a long couple of days, and I need some sleep. We'll talk more tomorrow." She nods in agreement. I stand up and head to the bedroom.

It's hard to believe it was just a couple days ago I was taping the victims of the mass shooting, chasing Patrick Newberry and capturing his death. Having those conversations with Roger and Aaron that made me doubt myself. All those thoughts of settling down, changing my lifestyle.

Think of the children. They are innocent in all this.

At the door, I turn around to Cho. "You know, these kids, they were just looking for a better life with their families. I want to help. I *have* to help."

Cho smiles. "I just make sure. You will do good work."

That doesn't bring much comfort. But the decision is made. I'm going for it.

"We'll start first thing in the morning, okay?" I nod at Cho, and she smiles back.

Chapter 31

I wake to the smell of brewing coffee.

Bright sunshine streams in through the small bedroom window. I glance out and see the mighty Pacific Ocean, whitecaps dancing on the dark blue waves. Already I feel calmer.

Throwing on a robe, I go out to the living room and find Cho in her usual spot in front of her computer. She has on a pale blue kimono today, and her damp hair looks freshly washed.

"I make you hot coffee." She gestures to the kitchen, where steaming java is emanating from a fancy black and silver machine on the counter, a mug next to it.

"Thanks." I fill the cup and pull a chair next to her. "What are you working on today?"

Cho's fingers fly across the keyboard, her short nails painted in many different colors.

"I find crypto theft for one client. Shutting down ransomware for another."

"It never ends, right?"

"No. Just gets trickier." She looks at me and smiles. "But I have my tricks, too."

She swivels her chair to face mine. "So, we begin? Where you want to start?"

"I need to reinstall Tor on my computer, refresh my VPN, then I'd like you to walk me through how to keep safe while exploring the deep web and darknet."

Cho nods.

"Then you show me what you have on the migrant kids being trafficked."

An hour later, and TOR, short for "The Onion Router," is up and running on my laptop.

Cho explains it's a free, open-source browser to surf the internet anonymously and keeps all traffic encrypted. She says it was originally developed by the U.S. Navy to allow anonymous online communication for military organizations. But the military dropped the project in 2006, and it's been handled by a nonprofit ever since.

Many big news operations like BBC News, ProPublica even Facebook have "onion sites" or dark web versions of their regular websites to provide news about important events. They look very similar to their regular internet sites.

She first showed me how to use TOR during our investigation into the Bangkok, Thailand sex trafficking ring we finally busted. I was able to use it to protect my sources who gave me the names and location—dark web and physical—of the traffickers.

But the dark web is also the preferred site for many unregulated websites, including pirated movies, black markets and worse.

Cho shows me how to find links that take me into some of the most depraved websites: sick, perverse types of pornography, which is huge money; suicide, child porn, drug trading, white supremacy and harassment.

"There are rumors of gladiator fights, where people battle to the death," Cho says. "Some say are 'human experiments' and if know where to look, can buy hitman. But most of those fake."

The "chans" links are some of the worst, with images that are impossible to unsee, and messages describing victims that sound as natural as talking about a girlfriend's makeup. Only much more graphic.

Trouble is, you can't just do a general search for "hitmen" or "sex traffickers." You need to identify the exact web address to visit a dark website, and the URLs are long gobbledygook combinations of random letters and numbers. Once you're there, the discussions happen in the forums.

My strong stomach can only take so much of those horrible websites before I tell Cho I need a break. I get more coffee.

Out the window above the kitchen sink is a stunning view of the ocean. *Being near water would be good.* I've always been drawn to the sea, the repetitive crashing waves always soothing. Los Angeles would be a good hub, or maybe San Diego. A quick trip to Coronado Island last year helped refresh my brain after covering a horrific train derailment that killed 20 people and injured more than 150.

The view helps take my mind off the troubling website images pulsing in my head. I gaze around her apartment, with its tiny kitchen table, small two-seater sofa and lots of personal items that make it home for Cho. The longing in my heart for a similar place of my own gets stronger.

"We stop for now." Cho stands from her seat, stretches. "Go for lunch, your favorite place, yes?"

Chapter 32

The rich smells of ginger, garlic, green onion and soy sauce take over my senses as we enter Chun Chinese, a classic Asian eatery in Venice Beach since the late 70s.

It's mostly packed with Asians, even at 11 in the morning. The space is small, but tables are arranged to maximize the square footage. Traditional red lanterns hang from the ceiling, and a red accent wall and napkins of the same color continue the theme.

Two sets of chopsticks are set at each seat. I remember my confusion last time I ate here with Cho, and she explained the outer set of chopsticks is used to serve yourself from the main bowl onto your own plate. Then you switch to the inside chopsticks to eat. That way the serving chopsticks stay clean and you don't pass germs.

On the menu there's a great mix of Mandarin and Szechuan dishes, and I can't wait to feast on their spicy Kung Pao squid. We start with Szechuan wonton soup and steamed dumplings, and sip hot tea in small cups while waiting for the main course.

"You like living in Los Angeles?" I ask.

Cho thinks for a moment. "Yes. Family here. Mother, father, two sisters, cousins. Never live anywhere else except China."

Family. I hardly remember what it was like living with my parents, and to live near them at this stage in my life seems foreign. Without any siblings, and not knowing what few second cousins are spread around the country, "family" has kind of a hollow sound to it for me.

And to only have lived in two places? While my parents were in the military, we moved every three years, sometimes more often, and I lost count after five moves from kindergarten to ninth grade that included Alabama, Texas and Alaska before finishing high school in Bitburg, Germany. *Guess that's how I'm able to travel so lightly now.*

"You move here?" Cho interrupts my thoughts. "We work together more," she says with a smile.

"Hmm… maybe. Thinking about it. I haven't had my own place in so long…"

"You got boyfriend? Want to settle down?"

"Uh, no steady boyfriend. Don't know if I'll ever really settle down. I—"

The arrival of our entrees interrupt that thought, and the hot dried chili peppers and onions tickle my nose. We dig in and are silent for a few minutes as the chopsticks fly.

I think about Aaron in New Mexico, and Roger in Atlanta. There was that brief fling with Bryan in New York City, and I've seen him a couple of times over the years, but he's not the settling-down type either. *Like I would recognize what that "type" looks like? That's a laugh.* And while I try not to think about Michael in Phoenix, his face appears in my mind. *Never again.*

I lean back in the red padded restaurant chair and sigh.

"That was fabulous." I wipe the spicy sauce off my mouth with a napkin.

Cho pushes a fortune cookie toward me. "Is good luck."

I break mine open and read aloud, "Look around. Happiness is trying to catch you." *"Between the sheets,"* I think to myself. The crass high school response would probably not be appreciated by Cho, so I don't say it out loud. But an image of Aaron and me in bed flashes through my brain.

But what will bring me happiness? It used to be my job, and that's all I thought I'd ever need. As I approach 40, I consider maybe it's an age thing which is bringing up these mixed thoughts and odd feelings. I shake it out of my head. *Enough of that for now.*

I wash the cookie down with a final sip of tea.

"Okay, I'm ready to get to work. So, how can we find out more about the migrant kids?"

"I work with group of hackers from South Korea on human trafficking, mostly forced labor," Cho says. "But they think they close to finding link to U.S. migrant sex houses. Large operation in Thailand, India and China. Recently started in U.S."

"Let's go see if they have something new."

Chapter 33

Back in Cho's apartment, her colorful fingernails quickly tapping the keyboard, and she's back in the dark web.

"Just who are these hackers?" I've switched to iced tea on this warm afternoon. "These are the potential middlemen you were talking about? Are they good guys or bad guys?"

Cho sticks out her bottom lip, considering. "Yes. Many good. But they need to make money, too."

"Thing is, if I get any information from them, I have to identify exactly who they are. I can keep them anonymous, but will they give me names?"

Cho looks at me doubtfully.

I continue. "Verification will also be tough. I'm not sure—"

My cell rings. It's Roger from News Crews International.

"'Scuse me a minute. I'd better take this."

I carry the phone into the bedroom. "Hey Rog, didn't expect to hear from you."

"You all right? Just wanted to see how you were doing with your research."

"I'm fine. Trolling the deep web, but no direct leads yet." I'm curious about his call. "You actually just checking in?"

"Are you in L.A.?"

Answering a question with a question. "Yes," I say hesitantly.

"All right. Full disclosure. It's a big one. Someone upstairs likes you, because somehow they managed to get you embedded on a sting operation of a huge drug bust going down after midnight tonight. Feds, SWAT, all the top dogs."

My adrenaline surges. These are rare, as no one wants the liability of a civilian on a dangerous mission. But a few in law enforcement now recognize the power of television to tell their story, and it helps keep their government budgets in the black. This will be the third sting I've been on, and certainly sounds like it may be the biggest.

He continues. "Bunch of businesses linked to money laundering for drug cartels. You said you wanted to be off, but..."

Here we go again. I try to focus on one mission, but the excitement mounts in anticipation of this job. *What is wrong with me? You can just say no.*

"Where in L.A.?"

"Does that mean you'll do it?"

I hesitate. *No, I guess you can't say no. Unable to pass up the exhilaration of exposing a drug ring.*

"Yes." I heave a sigh just for effect. "Give me the details."

"Great, thanks, TJ. Okay, it's downtown..."

He gives me the specifics, and my mind races as I consider the items I'll need: Kevlar vest, small camera, battery packs, phone charger, data cards.

After we hang up, I look over at the bedroom door. Cho stands there, a curious expression on her face.

"I know, I know, I said I was taking a break from news." I shrug my shoulders. "Once a news junkie, always a news junkie, I guess."

I pull items from my gear bag that I'll need. "It's not happening 'til 2 a.m., but I've gotta be at the FBI office tonight for a meeting at 6. Chances are I'll be back here for breakfast tomorrow morning."

Cho's eyebrows rise as if questioning my plans. Then she turns back to the main room.

I remove my gold necklace and tuck it inside my suitcase for safekeeping. I do five minutes of jump rope to get my adrenaline flowing.

I chastise myself on the drive to the FBI office.

You're all over the place. "Focus" is not in your vocabulary. Why can't you just concentrate on one thing at a time?

But no, a gig from Roger, especially this one, is like crack in your system. The adrenaline, the eagerness, getting the best shot, taking down the bad guys, it's like an addiction.

Stop it. Get your head in the game.

I've driven five miles in the black Mustang rental, but I don't remember a bit of it. I shake my head, willing the negative thoughts to disperse.

There'd probably be plenty of freelance jobs in Los Angeles if I were to get a place here. I wouldn't have to travel that much, just make this my base. I could work more with Cho—

"Damn!"

A white panel van swerves into my lane, and I brake. A quick glance behind me, and I'm grateful no one is too close.

You're gonna fuck this up if you don't get your shit together.

The GPS voice instructs me to turn into the lower-level parking garage of the Federal building.

This is your job. People count on you. It's time to bust some drug-running ass.

Chapter 34

Darkmover sits in a large, opulent office, relaxing with a small cordial glass of Romanian Țuică, a treat for a job well done.

The room's wingback chairs face a large bay window that overlooks downtown Bucharest. Bright red geraniums bloom from a flowerbox, and the sun slides down through a coral, yellow and lavender sky.

The rich plum taste of the country's preferred spirit is like lovemaking in the mouth.

A maid, dressed in black with a white apron, enters. *"Cina este aproape gata,"* she says in Romanian.

"Tsk, tsk, tsk, Cristina," Darkmover says without turning. "You know zee rules."

The woman bows her head. "Deener… almos' ready," she stammers.

"Ees better. Go."

The maid is waved away with a flick of a wrist.

Another sip as the strategy to infiltrate the United States of America is contemplated. Darkmover hums the song "You've Got a Friend."

Chapter 35

The boring beige conference room is full of law enforcement from various branches.

The only colors on the wall are from the round FBI and DEA seals, displayed front and center behind a podium.

Bureau agents stand out in their dark suits and white shirts. Drug enforcement personnel in casual jeans or khakis and polos pull on mesh vests with DEA on the back, their Kevlar vests bulging underneath. The word POLICE screams from the backs of Los Angeles Police Department officers' shirts.

When I enter the room wearing my PRESS vest, a few undercovers pull on thin black head coverings with eye cut-outs, so their covers won't be blown.

I check in with my contact.

"TJ Banks, News Crews International."

A female FBI agent eyes me suspiciously. She finds my name and inspects the press credentials hanging around my neck. She nods, but not without showing a little disdain.

"You'll be with Detective Jason Brightman from LAPD. The tall one over there."

She nods her chin toward a lanky man with wavy, shoulder-length brown hair chatting with a SWAT officer.

"Stay behind him at all times, do not get cocky and do everything he says. Got it?"

"Got it."

I head toward Brightman. *Good looking guy, probably 40s, nervous smile.* I stick out my hand. "I'm TJ Banks, NCI, covering the bust today."

Brightman gives a bit of a double-take and glances around the room briefly before his eyes settle back on mine. "Wait, I thought you were a, I mean, you're a girl, er, woman—" He ignores my outstretched arm. I lower it.

"I'm a journalist. Nice to meetcha. I'm here to record what goes down this morning and prove to the public their tax dollars are being well spent on your salaries."

Brightman's face flushes a bit, and it's not the first time someone, usually a man, has thought that "TJ Banks" is male, not female. *Duh. Did that on purpose, just for this reason.*

"Oh. Right. But this could go sideways. I can't guarantee—"

"I don't need a babysitter. You do what you do, and I'll do what I do. My instructions are to stick behind you, so I'll shoot over your shoulder and get as much footage as I can. Don't worry about me. I can take care of myself."

"Right. Okay." He gathers himself.

"What kind of drugs are you expecting to find today?"

"Uh, coke, fentanyl, China White H, plus cash, weapons. We believe—"

"All right, listen up everyone." A well-built man with a military flat top gets the room's attention with his powerful voice from a podium microphone at the front. I nod at Brightman and turn to the speaker.

"As most of you are aware, with the help of Europol, we've been watching an international drug operation dealing in various worldwide currencies and cryptocurrencies on the deep web. They've been using devices called Anon that they think are encrypted and keeps them anonymous… only we worked with the manufacturer to get this product on the black market and into their hands. We've been watching their chats, seeing their photos and following their deals."

"Like WhatsApp on steroids," one man quips, and chuckles sweep through the room.

"We're calling it Operation Black Buffer, and we anticipate finding 15 to 20 kingpin leaders of their U.S. drug operation along with a major cache of illegal substances, cash, guns, possibly jewelry and other luxury items. We expect them to be heavily armed and ready to put up a fierce resistance. We're hoping the element of surprise will tip the outcome in our favor."

"What kind of a building we goin' into?" asks an LAPD officer.

"It's a warehouse in South Central. Two-story, brick, few windows."

"How many ways out?" I ask, and feel all eyes shift to me, realizing many see me for the first time, and sending daggers my way. *Don't flinch.* I hold my gaze on the speaker.

"Large entrance at the front, small one on the side. We'll have them both covered, along with a window on the west side." He pauses and looks toward a group of drug enforcement agents. "Reminder to you DEA guys: this is one of the first times you'll be wearing body-worn cameras as part of the Justice Department's new program. Do NOT forget to turn on those BWCs as soon as you hit the ground."

Several of the agents fiddle with their cameras, adjusting them on the front of their chests. I make a mental note to make sure to get footage of the cameras, as the Justice program is just rolling out. I recall hearing a recent news conference with the attorney general, heads of the FBI, DEA and other agencies, all calling for "transparency and accountability." *Great, more competition for me.* But the quality of the footage will never be as good as mine.

Chapter 36

It's after hours in his spacious Albuquerque office as Aaron Porter combs through the computer for a few verified Bureau reports about trafficking of migrant children during the previous four to eight years.

One, a small group in the Albany, New York area, was suspected of having eight children aging in ranges from 9 to 13, who were being shopped for pornography and sex. It was thought to have three boys and five girls, but when agents from the NYC Bureau went in, the occupants had fled, seemingly during the middle of a meal. Fast-food wrappers with half-eaten burgers littered the kitchen table, and there were a few items of clothing and shoes were strewn about the tiny apartment. But nothing that could link the children to their parents. Or identify the traffickers.

Aaron received permission to investigate and contacted the FBI's Child Exploitation and Human Trafficking Task Force in New York. They are a dedicated bunch, and Aaron is looking forward to working with them.

His flight leaves first thing in the morning.

The agent powers down his laptop, gathers the cables and puts it all in a small carrying case. He takes a few files and straightens the top of desk. He turns off the light before locking the door.

I'll be on the opposite coast from TJ, he thinks randomly.

Chapter 37

There's enough pent-up energy and testosterone in the room to fill a football field as the time draws near for the sting op.

Detective Brightman and his team have been going over and over their part. Heated discussions erupt in other parts of the room as nerves are on edge. It's mostly men in the room, and the two other women I spot— one DEA and one FBI—aren't exactly giving me a sense of camaraderie.

I begin to realize that while Brightman is in charge of the LAPD officers, he may not be going in where the action is. *Last thing I want is to be standing outside with nothing to tape.*

"So, Detective, who exactly will be going into the warehouse?"

"SWAT will take the lead, with a couple of our LAPD tactical guys, then DEA and FBI."

"And where will *you* be?"

"In a command position."

"You mean *outside* the building, *inside* a vehicle?" My sarcasm gets the best of me. I want to say *I'm here to work, not eat popcorn and watch a show.* But I don't want to piss him off.

"You got a problem with that?"

"No, sir."

He continues the conversation with his officers. I appear to listen, but I'm also trying to hear what the SWAT guys are planning. I want to be where the action is, and they would be it.

Now, how to follow them? Probably too late to get reassigned to someone else. I could jeopardize my position on this operation, which might affect whomever it is in my upper food chain who got me here, and then ruin it for other journalists who want to cover similar busts.

Oh, and I suppose there's a risk of getting hurt, but that's low on my totem pole.

Do I follow the rules or follow the footage?

I'm given permission to videotape some aspects of the meeting.

While many clam up when I get close, I'm able to listen in on some of the plans by the different agencies. My strategy develops.

It's 12:30 a.m., go time.

My heart beats a little faster as I hoist on my gear backpack. I feel clammy with perspiration under my Kevlar vest, and not all because of its thickness.

I pull a black knit cloth cover with a lens opening around my video camera so the glass is the only thing that could reflect. It's got a lightweight aluminum rig that holds a short microphone with a furry windscreen, a small external monitor and right side and top side handles.

Camera recording on my shoulder, I grab a bottle of water from a cooler as I follow Brightman and the others down the hall. We pack into the elevators to submerge to the basement where the vehicles are lined up and ready to move. We file into a large, unmarked, probably bulletproof van, taking seats on the two flat benches on either side of the hardened steel cargo area. For security, there are no windows, but I spot the baffled roof air vents that obstruct a direct line of fire into the truck.

It reminds me of a series of armored truck heists I covered a couple of years ago.

In one case, two guards were picking up cash from a large bank in New York City, during the middle of the day. The driver survived the carefully timed ambush, but the second guard, the hopper, who carries valuables to and from the truck, was shot and killed just before he was able to put the $1 million in large currencies inside the drop safe.

Before the driver could react, a huge drone swooped in, picked up the bag and flew off, never to be seen again.

I take deep breaths to keep the adrenaline at bay, for now. We ride in silence.

Chapter 38

According to my watch, it's been about a half hour drive by the time we get to South Central L.A., a huge warehouse district.

Although it's dark when we get out, heavily graffitied block walls and buildings stretch away on either side, and trash blows at our feet in the late-night breeze.

A block away from the building, the other vehicles pull in along the street, and the occupants quietly emerge.

Brightman speaks, low. "Banks. You're with me."

My camera out and recording again, I nod and follow him to another large black and white truck with "Los Angeles Police Department Mobile Command Post" on the side. Two pop-outs on either side open silently. A large satellite antenna, similar to ones on the live news trucks I've worked in, glides up about 10 feet in the air.

Inside, it also looks like the mobile vehicles the cable news and most large television stations use. There's a large wall of eight different screens, all flickering to life. Another wall is the engineering equipment hub, with cables plugged into audio, video, internet and other metal boxes. Brightman points me to a conference table in the center, with telephones and built-in charging pods. I set my half-full bottle of water in front of a chair nearest the door but continue to stand and shoot.

The monitors receive pictures from the various body cameras as well as a wide shot of the scene, presumably from the top of the command post truck. It's not bad video. In fact, the quality is better than I expected it would be, especially in the dark. *Sure, I can videotape the screens, and it would be decent footage. But I still want to be where the real action is. My eyes, my professional high-definition shots, not their jiggly low-res ones. Plus, I want to see the looks on the faces of the drug kingpins when they get taken down.*

Voices get more animated inside the truck and through audio speakers from outside as the sting start time nears. The nervous energy is thrilling and contagious.

An LAPD captain, judging from the pair of silver bars on his uniform, adjusts his headset over his short, graying hair. A little bead of perspiration glows on his forehead.

"SWAT, are you a go?"

"10-4, SWAT is go," a voice crackles.

"DEA, report."

"DEA is a go," another voice answers.

The rest of the agencies check in, and there's a palpable electricity as the mission is about to begin.

All eyes in command post are glued to the monitors, including Brightman's. I slide silently toward the door, getting a wide shot of the scene. *Red recording light blinking. Deep breaths. Steady shot.*

"On my command," the captain continues. "In three... two... one. Go, go, go!"

The room is filled with frenzied voices from those outside the truck, repeating the command. I slip out the back door, unseen.

Chapter 39

As my heart pounds, I sprint toward a group of SWAT agents and fall in behind them, still recording.

One man glances over his shoulder at me for a second with a curious look on his face but continues running toward the large front entrance.

I can tell my pupils are dilated from the increase in adrenaline, as things look brighter despite the dark night. I get a tight shot of a battering ram as it pounds the metal door, and an LAPD officer pries open the door with a long hooked tool I've seen used for forcible entry by law enforcement. The door gives way and agents yell as they enter.

"LAPD! FBI! DEA!" multiple voices shout as they stream in. I'm almost to the entrance myself, and through my viewfinder, capture a couple of men inside trying to run, their eyes wide with surprise and fright.

I want to stay out of the way, so I stop just outside the entrance and continue to shoot. What appears to be large bundles of wrapped substances—probably drugs—line one side of the interior wall. I videotape another wall holding a variety of weapons. There's a folding table with five straight chairs around it, two on their sides, and files and papers strewn on the floor. I'd love to get a close-up of the papers, but out of the corner of my eye, at the smaller side exterior entrance, the door opens.

"Freeze! FBI!"

I swing my camera around and jog toward the agents covering that door. *What is sticking out of the—*

Guns!

Suddenly a spray of bullets erupts from inside the building and a couple of agents fall to the ground.

The zing of a bullet whizzes by my head and I feel something hot and burning on my leg. *Fuck! Am I hit?* I slam to the asphalt parking lot with the other agents as gunfire is returned, but I manage to get my camera pointed back where the gunfire came from, looking through the viewfinder now. I don't have time to think about the pain in my calf as I train my lens, still a little wobbly, on two men in green and brown camouflage, bulletproof vests and black helmets in the doorway facing me, both wielding heavy duty machine guns.

One head turns my way. *Is he looking at me? Can he see me?* I freeze.

Reinforcements from the front cautiously file along the side of the building. A DEA agent fires from the ground and the two camo guys fire back. Agents who have been struck groan in pain.

I sense momentary confusion as the agents outside determine their next plan of attack. There's gunfire from inside the building and the two camo men go down.

"Clear!" comes from several voices inside the warehouse as they secure the structure.

I keep rolling video, even though my leg is throbbing and my teeth crunch with grit from dirt in my mouth.

Sirens wail up the street, and I swing my camera that way to capture emergency medical responders from red Los Angeles Fire Department vehicles as they roll up and burst out the doors. I pan the camera back toward the fallen law enforcement officers, some picking themselves up, as the paramedics run into the shot to attend to the injured agents. *This is freakin' amazing footage. Those scumbags are going away for a long—*

"Banks! What the fuck?"

Chapter 40

I get hauled back to the command post.

How the hell am I going to explain this to Roger, and Aaron, if he hears about it? I seriously don't feel that much pain and I take the severe tongue lashing with lots of f-words by Detective Brightman.

It's at least five minutes into his tirade about me being a civilian, disobeying orders, blah blah blah, before he realizes there's blood running down my dark jeans and pooling on the floor under my black boot. I'm saved from further admonishment when a medic who introduces himself as Ryan is called in to work on my injury.

He's stocky, with huge biceps and thighs, and short light brown hair. Ryan takes scissors and cuts through my black pants leg to expose where a bullet skimmed the side of my calf.

"You're lucky," he says. "It's just a flesh wound."

He cleans it, which stings like hell, puts a couple of butterfly strips over the flesh and covers it with a gauze pad.

"Can you walk?"

I stand. "Sure, I'll be fi—" but the room starts spinning, and my legs feel weak. Ryan grabs me and sits me back down.

"I just stood up too fast. Give me a couple of minutes."

My hands shake and feel a little damp, and sweat rolls down my spine, despite having taken off my hot Kevlar vest.

"Put your head between your legs," a faraway voice says.

I comply. The swimming in my head settles down.

Adrenaline is a funny thing.

I'm aware it's technically a chemical "fight or flight" response, when faced with trauma. The strong hormone floods the body to help the nervous system respond to stress or danger. Blood flow increases, sugar is pumped into the bloodstream, all to help the body deal more effectively with whatever threat looms.

Those who love adrenaline highs—skydivers, zipliners, racecar drivers—crave the thrill they feel when epinephrine is released.

Others, such as police officers, firefighters, military personnel, rescue workers and first responders, are routinely subjected to adrenaline surges during emergencies and disasters. Sometimes daily.

Journalists are on both lists, but we are often considered the last of those groups to recognize the psychological implications of repeated adrenaline surges and the aftermath.

The first thing that happens is blood sugar drops, which causes the shakiness and weakness. It can take up to an hour for adrenaline to subside, and since it also stimulates dopamine in the nervous system, I usually feel great afterwards.

That is not the case this time, because of the added shock from the bullet wound. And because of the shitload of trouble I'm in.

It's a little after 4 in the morning by the time I manage to get out of the command post.

The last thing I want to do is ride back to the Federal building in the bulletproof vehicle with the other officers, many of whom are none too happy with me. So, I call a rideshare to take me back to Cho's. I figure I'll pick up the rental car tomorrow. Er, later today.

The driver doesn't mind going through a fast-food restaurant for me, as I'm starving. That's another aftermath of adrenaline. I polish off two of the four sausage, egg and cheese sandwiches in the car, which taste so incredibly good. I buy him a cup of coffee.

I try to let myself in quietly to Cho's apartment, but she's in her chair, a steaming cup of hot tea in her hand.

"Told you I'd be back for breakfast," I quip. "Brought you an egg sandwich."

Cho's smile becomes a frown as she does a doubletake as I get closer. She notices the dirt and grime plus my tattered jeans and bandaged leg.

"What happen? You okay?"

"Yeah, I'll be fine. Just a little scratch."

Technically, I'm feeling more pain now that my body's nervous system returns to normal. *Won't be jumping rope for a few days.*

"Hey, I'm gonna take a shower, then I gotta call my news op and send them some footage. It was an incredible sting operation, even though three officers were injured. But the good guys managed to get all the bad guys and even killed a couple of them. And I am the only one with footage."

I'm feeling just a bit too proud at the moment, and the apprehension on Cho's face causes me to tamp down my euphoria.

"Yeah, well, uh, I mean… I'll see you in a bit."

I wolf down the rest of my third sandwich as I head to the bedroom. I stop and turn around sheepishly. "Cho, may I borrow a couple of things?"

The hot water feels great as it pounds on my shoulders, my neck, my back.

A garbage sack and duct tape cover my bandage, and my leg really aches now.

Once I'm out of the shower, exhaustion overpowers my body. Is that the result of post-adrenaline decline? Or is my age showing? *Don't go there.*

I'll upload some raw footage, grab a couple hours of sleep and put together a package later. I doubt there's been any news of the sting operation yet, so a quick nap will help me concentrate.

The silk sheets and down comforter on Cho's bed feels fabulously soft on my skin as I drift off to sleep.

Chapter 41

It's afternoon on the East Coast, and News Crews International Vice President Steven Godfrey is in his office, his size 13 black Gucci loafers propped up on his cherrywood desk, as he flips through TikTok videos of scantily clad dancing women.

His secretary's voice comes on the intercom. "Line two, Mr. Godfrey. Washington, DC," a woman says.

"Thanks, Marlene." He flicks off the app, lowers his feet and picks up the telephone handset. "Steven Godfrey here."

"Congratulations on that drug bust in Los Angeles, Godfrey. Well done," a nasal voice intones.

"Charlie! Good to hear from you. Thanks for the lead, yes, that was some great footage, wasn't it?"

"And that reporter, let's see, TJ Banks, is it? She's a gutsy gal."

"Right? It was quite serendipitous meeting you at the White House Correspondents Dinner. As a government official, your finger seems to be on the pulse of what's coming down the pike." *If I suck up to this guy, maybe we'll land another exclusive.*

"I feel the news media has an important role to play, and in my position at DHHS, I always like knowing what types of stories you are interested in," Charlie says. "I've been watching that Banks woman since she covered the shooting of the Congressional baseball team when they got fired on a few years ago."

"Hey, good memory. So, you got something else for us?"

"Indeed, I do. And I think that Banks woman would be perfect for it."

"Great, whaddaya have?"

Chapter 42

The noise of heavy gunfire seems to be all around me.

My heart pounds with a sense of panic as I realize the bullets are blasting right through me. The anxiety wakes me with a start, as the shooting dream morphs into a light tapping on the bedroom door.

"Yeah, come in." I feel groggy, like in slow motion.

The door opens and Cho pokes her head in. "Is almost 10 a.m. You still want to sleep?"

"What?!" I suddenly register the midmorning sun streaming through the bedroom window. "Oh, shit, I had no idea I was out so long." I swing my feet out of the bed and start to stand, but the bullet graze on my leg shouts its reluctance. "Oww…"

"I help you?" Cho asks timidly.

"No, sorry, I'm good. Wow, I slept hard. Thanks for waking me up." I inch up a little more cautiously this time, and while my muscles are sore from the top down, I manage a good stretch. "Got any coffee?"

"Of course." Cho disappears back into the main room.

I move more sluggishly than normal as I get dressed. *Was it all worth it? Am I pushing my limit—and my luck?* Seems like it wasn't long ago when I could take on any morbid crime story and bounce right back to cover a traumatic accident without skipping a beat. Now I'm behind schedule, as I need to look through all the footage, pick the best shots from the drug bust, create a full story package and upload it to Roger. At this point, it'll probably be noon by the time I'm done.

Not good.

Next time, just say no. Focus.

Concentrating only on sex traffickers can keep me plenty busy, and with as much as is happening in the United States, I wouldn't even have to travel too far anymore. Spend time on the computer, handle logistics with Roger, then cover the occasional bust. Forget this running from crime to crime. Been there, done that, tired of it.

I slip out the video card from my camera and head to Cho's "office."

She's quiet as I get a cup of coffee and insert the card into my laptop. But as soon as the footage downloads, I get another twinge of excitement, that damned adrenaline teasing my body again. The thrill and excitement of the drug operation is like cocaine in my system, and I realize I love what I do.

Or my body is just addicted to the exhilarating sensation.

Chapter 43

I piece together a 3-minute, 45-second story—longer than the standard 1 minute 30, but they told me to go for it—with only video and natural sound.

The agents storm the building. Suspects try to flee. Gunfire. Agents down. More gunfire. Medics arrive. Agents lead suspects away.

On the video, I can pinpoint the exact moment my leg is hit with the bullet. That's another funny thing adrenaline can do: mask the pain. I dropped to the ground like the other agents, still taping, and it wasn't until much later when the powerful hormone started wearing off that I felt the burning effects of the gunshot wound.

I also send Roger additional clips of raw video and sound a news organization could use with their own voiceover. It's almost 1 and I'm suddenly famished.

"Hey, Cho, you wanna order in lunch?"

Cho's fingers fly across her keyboard. She is intent on whatever cyber project she's working on. She finishes and looks up. "Yes. But you may want to see this first."

I hobble toward her and look over her shoulder. I can tell Cho is in a chat room on the deep web.

I don't remember the names and acronyms of the various software Cho uses, but I recognize The Onion Router browser, which she's operating on a virtual machine for protection and privacy purposes. She also has a link-analysis tool to keep track of and preserve evidence, to be able to prove where she found her information. She tells me it's critical for what could potentially result in a court case.

Banner ads pulse and flash with gaudy graphics advertising different chat rooms and marketplaces. Cho moves her cursor to point to a conversation in a sex trafficking site.

"I monitor this chat about migrant kids. There's reference to trafficking house in Arizona."

"Where in Arizona?"

"Phoenix."

Phoenix. Michael. My heart races a bit at the thought of his name. I reach for my necklace, but feel my bare neck, realizing I haven't put it back on yet. *Snap out of it.* "That makes about five you've found around the country. Any more details?"

"I see one name repeated: Darkmover. Mean anything to you?"

"No, you?"

"I think perhaps that is person heading up big operation. Seems to be much respect for this Darkmover."

"How can we find out who he is?"

"I continue to search. I will inform you."

"How about if I jump on and pose as a trafficker? Maybe we can sniff him out that way."

Cho shakes her head. Without words, her face clearly says *Don't even try it.*

"Okay, okay, too soon. I'll see if my FBI sources are aware of Darkmover."

And figure out what to do about Michael if I go to Phoenix.

Chapter 44

Steven Godfrey, Vice President of Newsgathering for NCI, gazes out the gold curtained window, not really seeing the view of the Potomac from his Alexandria, Virginia high-rise office for News Crews International.

It's furnished with gold fabric chairs, gold pulls on the high-end wood desk and filing cabinets. Lush gold carpet completes the elegant room.

He strides to his desk and punches a button on the telephone set. "Marlene, get Roger Lester in Atlanta on the horn."

"Yes, sir," comes the answer through the speakerphone.

"And bring me a cup of coffee."

"Yes, sir," Marlene replies.

Godfrey turns back to stare out the window, a scant sun amidst the clouds.

His desk phone beeps.

"Roger Lester on the line," Marlene says.

Godfrey picks up the receiver. "Roger, how ya doin' today?"

"Uh, just fine, Mr. Godfrey, how are you?" Roger says.

"Never better. And call me Steve. How's our Georgia team?"

"Well, everyone is good, working hard, sir. Is there something I can do for you?"

"I wanted to check up on that freelancer we've got, TJ Banks? You convinced her to become a full timer for NCI yet?"

"Um, no sir. I think she prefers freelance."

"Well, you keep working on her, okay? She's one rising star. I don't understand how she can stand to shoot all the gory stuff she does, like that Albuquerque mall massacre, but sure glad she does."

A petite blonde, carrying a tray of coffee and condiments, delivers a beverage to Godfrey's desk. He barely nods, and she leaves, as Godfrey dumps two spoonfuls of sugar and a heavy stream of cream in the white mug. He takes a sip.

"Did she like that drug sting gig? She sure got some amazing footage."

"She did appreciate the assignment. TJ got hit with a bullet in her leg, but she's doing fine."

Godfrey's eyes go wide. His legs threaten to go out from under him, but he catches the edge of his desk and sits. "Did she?" *He had heard she was injured, but didn't know she got hit with a bullet!* He recovers and blows out a breath. "Well, she's one tough cookie." Godfrey takes another slurp of coffee. "I might have a big extortion case I think she'd like. She could use all her undercover 'lipstick cams' and other secret stuff."

"I can ask her, but TJ is taking some time off from regular assignments to follow a specific story."

Godfrey jumps to his feet. "What? How much 'time off' does she need?"

"She asked for a month."

"Well, shit. What's the story? We gonna get it?"

"I don't have a lot of details, but it's one of her pet projects: sex trafficking."

Godfrey puts one hand in his pants pocket. "Ugh. That's never great footage. Crying victims in shadows, no names. Talk to her about this extortion thing, wouldja? I think she'd do a helluva job."

"I can try, Mr. Godfrey, but don't hold your breath."

"It's Steve, call me Steve."

"So, Steve, if I may ask, where are you getting these leads?"

"Oh, now, Rog, you know I can't reveal my sources," he says with a hearty laugh. "You just work on TJ and leave the rest to me."

Godfrey hangs up the phone. From his desktop, he picks up a professional headshot photo of TJ Banks, with a serious stare at the camera, and smiles as he continues to drink his coffee.

Chapter 45

It's early evening East Coast time as Aaron Porter sits in a small office cubicle, his temporary space while he works in the New York Bureau on the migrant child trafficking case.

His shirt sleeves are rolled up, and his jacket is tossed over an extra chair. The counters are bare except for his laptop, cell phone, empty in and out boxes and an open tin of cinnamon mints.

The Task Force team gave a full briefing on the suspected Albany, New York trafficking house first thing this morning. Among the items found in the cramped space believed to be used to hold children was a small piece of crumpled paper with a phone number and, in Spanish, *jefe* or "boss." When they called, it went to what was probably a burner phone, but agents were attempting to track whatever history they could.

Aaron scrutinizes the computer photos from the last known whereabouts of the traffickers, trying to find anything that could further identify the people using these children for their own profits. The thought makes his blood boil.

He zooms in on a distinctive pair of kids' shoes—the kind with rollers on the bottom and colorful lights along the side—and wonders whether there's any information from a parent's description to match with a missing child. *Yeah, like trying to find a specific cactus spine in the desert.*

"You Porter?" A woman in a blue suit coat, pants and white shirt leans into Aaron's cubby, a pink note in her hand.

Aaron looks up and nods.

"This just came in from the L.A. Bureau. Something about an acquaintance of yours who's been shot." She looks at the paper. "Banks?"

Aaron clenches his jaw, but he tries not to show any emotion on his face. He reaches for the message. "Thanks, appreciate it."

"Sure." The woman leaves.

Aaron's hands turn clammy as he reads the note from a Bureau colleague who helped him get the Albuquerque position a few years ago.

L.A. Bureau drug op last night with DEA, LAPD, SWAT. Four injured with gunshot wounds including 2 DEA, 1 SWAT and 1 civilian reporter, TJ Banks. Think you know her?
John

Oh, god, he thinks, his heart tumbling as he fears the worst. He realizes his feelings for her go deeper each time her name and face flash through his brain.

Wait. It said injured, not dead. A bit of relief flows through his chest.

His next thought is: *What the hell has she gotten herself into this time?*

He picks up his cell phone, scrolls to TJ Banks in his contacts and presses "call," unconsciously crunching a breath mint as he waits.

The phone rings three times, then he hears TJ's voice, husky. "Banks." He closes his eyes at the sound. *Alive. Strong. Answering her phone.*

"It's Porter. What the hell?" he demands.

Chapter 46

Porter hears silence on the other end.

Then it sounds like TJ is stretching, maybe just waking up. "Hey, I was just about to call you."

He blows out the breath he didn't realize he had been holding. *She sounds like herself. When she's skirting the law, that is.* "Yeah, right. What happened?"

"Nothing really. I'm fine. Just a little flesh wound. No one killed, except the bad guys of course, and your team was amazing. They really—"

"Don't sugar coat it with me, Banks." He wants to be a tough guy but feels so thankful she wasn't badly hurt. "You got hit?"

"Yeah, on my calf. Hardly felt a thing. Well, not until later anyway. Got bandaged up and am good to go."

There's a pause on both sides. "All right." Porter's voice is low and husky, filled with more emotion than he expects.

"Aww, Porter, there you go again. If I didn't know any better, I'd think you might actually care," TJ quips. Her voice softens. "I appreciate your concern, really. I'm okay."

Aaron clears his throat. "You still in L.A.?"

"Right. Getting the lowdown on the deep and dark web, chasing traffickers. Might be heading to Phoenix, as Cho found a possible migrant child sex-trafficking house there. Maybe I can stop through Albuquerque after?"

He sits back in his chair. "I'm not there. I'm in New York."

"Oh. How come?"

"I got some intel about your migrant child trafficking case. I'm working with the Bureau's Child Exploitation and Human Trafficking Task Force here. They were right on top of a house with several children, but these people move fast."

"Aaron, that's amazing."

She rarely calls me by my first name. It sounds good.

"What can you tell me about it?" she asks.

He fills her in, and he senses she is grateful he's taking her seriously.

"That's why I was about to call you," TJ says. "We've found a reference to someone called 'Darkmover.' He may be a kingpin in the biz. Ever heard of him?"

Aaron sits up and grabs a pen, jotting down the name. "No, but I haven't worked trafficking for a while. Let me see what I can find out."

"Thanks. Let's… keep in touch. About this case, I mean."

"Of course. But Banks, you need to be very cautious. These guys are ruthless and will stop at nothing."

"I get it." Her voice is soft, as if chastised.

"Look, I'll put in a call to a friend of mine in the Phoenix office. Get in touch with her when you're in town."

"Thanks, Porter, that's great. Just text me her name."

Back to my last name. But it's still good to hear.

"Maybe you can come to Phoenix, too? It would be good to work together with you again."

Her voice deepens and sounds as if "work" isn't the only thing she'd like to do. A tingle in his groin reminds him of the same thing. "Maybe. I'll be in touch."

"Thanks, Porter."

"Be careful out there."

"Will do. Talk later."

Aaron hangs up the phone and closes his eyes. He sees TJ's face at the bar, red lips moving toward him and ending in a powerful kiss. In his office, her blue eyes, inches away, staring so intently into his. At his house, as they were making love, moaning, eyes closed. And at the restaurant, brave yet terrified at the same time, ready to run out of his life.

He runs a hand over his short-cropped hair. *Get back to work. No sense dwelling on what—or whom—you don't fully understand.*

He turns back to his computer and types, searching the Bureau's files for "Darkmover." Nothing comes up, and he knows he needs to drill down further. He pops another breath mint and settles in for a long search.

Chapter 47

I end the call with Aaron, noting it's mid-afternoon in Los Angeles.
I had only intended to nap for 30 minutes or so, but it's been three hours and I still feel like crap. I lean back onto the cushioned headboard of Cho's bed.

I close my eyes and see Aaron's face. At the bar, his dark eyes meeting, beckoning mine. In his office, one moment angry with me, the next wanting me. At his house, sleeping soundly, peacefully. And at the restaurant, eyes probing into mine, trying to uncover memories I've long since buried.

I think he cares about me, and the feeling is almost mutual, which scares the shit outta me. And he took my mind off Michael… until now.

Enough. You've got work to do. Traffickers to catch.

My cell rings again, but when I pick it up, the screen reads "unknown number." I ignore it and lean back again. *If it's not a telemarketer, they'll leave a message.*

I rest for a few more minutes, then realize I've got to get up and get back to work. As I swing my legs around to stand, my calf twinges with pain, and I steady myself against the bed. I smell Chinese takeout from the other room, and my watering mouth supersedes the stinging from the wound.

I pull out my gold necklace from its secure spot in the bag, and place it around my neck, straightening the diamond into the center.

Michael.

I limp out of the bedroom into Cho's world and several small white food boxes are lined up on the kitchen table. She stares at her monitor, chopsticks in her right hand deftly carrying rice and her du jour selection to her mouth from a bowl in her left.

"That smells amazing, Cho."

"Help yourself." She nods her head toward the food. "Everything okay?"

I pile rice, shrimp and noodles into a bowl, pour on shoyu and pick up chopsticks. "Yes." *How much do I tell Cho? We're friends, but we're so different. Would she understand the decisions I'm being faced with?* I fill a glass with ice and pour soda from the fridge.

"And no." I sit on a chair near her and take a bite. "That was my FBI... uh, contact." *What do I call him? Friend? Lover?* "He's a little pissed at me for getting hurt... yet he's in New York working on the migrant trafficking kids. He's going to see if he can find anything on Darkmover."

"That sound good, yes?" Cho rests her chopsticks in the bowl to take a sip of her tea.

"Yeah, it is. It's just that..." *What is it, really? Why can't I put it into words? Maybe because I don't have a grip on "it" myself.*

"You like him, yes? He like you, yes? Everything okay." It was a statement this time.

I swallow. *How is she able to boil it down so simply? But wait, it's not that simple. In fact, it's very complicated in so many ways.* "Well, yes, but... I'm going through some things... and it's been a long time since I've had a real relationship." I pause to look at Cho closely. *I haven't heard her speak of a significant other, nor have I seen any sign of one.* "How about you, Cho? Do you have a boyfriend?"

Cho gazes out the kitchen window and gets a faraway look in her eyes. "I have special friend once, long ago. We happy." A loving smile spreads over her face but fades within a couple of seconds. "But she get cancer and die. Now I rather be alone."

My heart tugs at this information. "I'm so sorry, Cho. But you're young. You could meet someone else."

She shakes her head. "Could never compare." Then she looks deep into my eyes. "What about you? What you afraid of?"

Chapter 48

Aaron asked me the same thing.

Now I realize I'm screwed when these same phrases keep getting repeated to me by different people.

I gather up the empty food boxes and put them in the trash. "Darn good question. Wish I knew the answer." *I call BS on myself.* "Yeah, that's bullshit. The answer's pretty simple. Classic case of not wanting to get my heart stomped on again."

"So, what happen?" Cho asks. "I good listener." She raises her eyebrows and smiles.

"Like I'm the only one this has ever happened to." I take a swig of my drink. "I worked with a great guy, Michael, at a small affiliate TV station in North Carolina. He was a reporter, I was a photographer, we worked together all the time and one thing led to another." I smile. "We understood each other's crazy schedules, and made it work. We talked about getting married, but we didn't know where our careers might take us.

"Then he got a new job in Phoenix. Shortly after that I went to Atlanta and started freelancing. We maintained the long-distance relationship and I thought it was actually working. I mean, he surprised me with a ring one Valentine's Day.

"But outta the blue he calls to say he's met someone else. I was blindsided. Then he told me I could keep the ring. This is the diamond from it." I finger the stone on the gold chain around my neck. "I felt so vulnerable and said, 'Never again.'

"So, I've been pouring myself into work ever since. I still meet a lot of men, but sex is on my terms. I mean, if men can have a woman in every port, why can't I?" *Not feeling so proud of that these days, however.* "And now Michael is a big shot news anchor in Phoenix. If I go there, do I contact him? Do I see him? How I can be in the same city and not think about him?"

"You believe he thinking of you?" Cho asks.

That stops me cold. I blink. *Why would I be on his mind? He's got a new wife, and according to his Facebook page I'm stalking, a baby. He's moved on—*

"Huh." I smile, realizing. "No, I'm sure he's moved on, which is what I need to do." I chuckle. "You're good, Cho. Ever think about being a therapist?"

Cho shrugs her shoulders. And there's her wry smile again. "But your FBI man... different?"

"He's far from *my* man." *Or is he? You're thinking about him a lot. You've let him in a little. And those eyes...* "But yes, he's different. I have feelings for him, but I'm terrified of getting hurt again, so I just take off."

"You keep running, maybe never be happy. Remember fortune cookie? 'Look around. Happiness trying to catch you.'"

"Yeah, like to snare me and break my heart again."

"Not just negative word." Cho types on the computer and reads. "Synonym of catch is 'someone desirable.' Gem. Prize. Treasure." She looks back to me. "You good catch, TJ. You good person. You work hard. You have good heart. FBI man know that."

I feel a lump in my throat, and my eyes start to fill. *Is that true? Do I deserve to be happy? Could I be happy again with someone like Aaron?*

"Thanks, Cho. That means a lot." I reach over and give her a hug.

Both our computers *ding-ding-ding* with alerts.

Chapter 49

Cho and I each turn to our devices.

"I got a hit on a message I left in one of the chats," I say.

Cho glares at me with an "I told you not to do that" look.

"Yeah, yeah. I only said I was looking for young girls, and that I have a buyer. Someone sent me a reply with a link to another chat room. What do you have?"

Cho looks back at her computer. "May have address for Phoenix house."

"That's awesome, Cho. Aaron—I mean, Agent Porter—gave me the name of an FBI contact there. Let me reach out to her and see if we can negotiate something."

"Okay, TJ."

I take my laptop to the bedroom so I won't bother Cho as I call Aaron's contact, Toni Karls, in the Phoenix FBI office.

There's a voicemail from that unknown number. Turns out it's a long-winded message from some vice president at NCI, Godby or Godfrey or something. *Who the hell is he?* At this point, I don't really care, but I save the message and dial the FBI agent's office.

"Karls," a curt voice answers.

"Agent Karls, this is TJ Banks, a… colleague of Special Agent Aaron Porter's out of Albuquerque." *Yeah, so we kinda work together, so we're kinda colleagues.*

"Yes, I am acquainted with Porter," she says, a bit suspiciously.

"I am working on a child sex-trafficking case and wondered if I could meet with you. I may have some information regarding Phoenix."

"What case is this? And who are you exactly?"

Oh boy, here we go.

"I'm a broadcast journalist, and I've worked on a number of sex-trafficking cases where I've been able to videotape the capture of the traffickers."

There's silence on the other end. I plunge ahead.

"Agent Porter is currently working with your CEHT task force in New York on one of several instances where migrant children separated from their parents at the border are not in foster homes but are being trafficked instead. I'm working with a cyber investigator in Los Angeles, and we believe we've found a similar house in Phoenix."

"Ms. Banks, we are aware of a number of reported trafficking rings here. There's nothing you—"

"We believe we have an exact address."

More silence.

"May I meet with you? I'm in L.A. now, but can be there first thing tomorrow morning."

"Why don't you just give me the address? We'll take it from there," Agent Karls says.

"I also have other information I think you'll be very interested in. I'd rather share it all in person." I pause. "Look, I understand how delicate these cases are, and I believe I can be of assistance. Agent Porter can vouch for my work."

"I will need to confirm it with him."

"Of course, I understand."

She's silent for a moment. "I can see you tomorrow at 10 a.m. in my office."

"Thank you, Agent Karls. I look forward to meeting you."

Yes! I'm in.

I go to the Southwest Airlines website and look for flights to Phoenix. They leave about every hour or so, and there appear to be plenty of seats available. *Let's see, if I return the rental car by 7, I can catch the 8 a.m. flight and be there by 9.* I make a seat reservation. I can book another rental car and make the short drive to her office in the north part of Phoenix by 10.

It should be great weather there, so I look at the "exotic" cars offered and pick a beautiful navy-blue Porsche Boxster convertible. It's $3,025 a week, but I made a bundle on the Albuquerque shoot as well as the drug sting, so I'm feeling flush. After all, what the hell do I spend my money on? There's no rent to pay, no car payment so no auto insurance. *Maybe that's another reason not to get stuck in one place. Think of all the money I'm saving living the life of a nomad.*

I complete the reservation, pick up my laptop and go back out to the living room to update Cho, who types furiously on her keyboard.

"Hey, Cho, I—"

She cuts me off with a "one minute" gesture, her index finger in the air.

I come around to her side as she writes a message in the same darknet chat room she found earlier.

C: *I pay $500 Ethereum but only if address legit.*

X: *Deal. Will send pgp link for deets.*

"Is that about the Phoenix address?" I ask incredulously.

Cho leans back. "Maybe. We see." Her brow is furrowed, as if worried.

"Keep track of everything I owe you." Now it's my turn for concern. "But I don't know much about cryptocurrency, and I don't have any."

"No problem. U.S. dollars good. I send you bill." She still looks very serious.

"Thanks. And perfect timing, because I'm heading to Phoenix tomorrow morning to meet with the FBI."

"As soon as I get address on PGP, I send to you same way."

I study Cho's face. "Something wrong, Cho?"

She takes both hands and smooths out her long, straight hair. "Getting closer to bad government people."

"That's good, right?" Realizing. "Wait, people?"

"May be more than one."

Chapter 50

I sit down to contemplate the implications.

"As in two? Or more?"

Cho shrugs her shoulders. "Don't know."

"It could be like that Jeffrey Epstein sex trafficker guy, who had all kinds of men and women helping him lure in young girls to molest. I guess it's naïve to think one person could be solely responsible for siphoning theses migrant kids into trafficking homes, monitoring them, potentially buying and selling them…" *The thought sickens me.*

"Must be careful." Cho turns her chair toward me. "What message you get in chat room?"

I open my computer and find the note. "Somebody called *lookforfun335* sent me a link to another discussion room. Should I click on it?"

"Wait." Cho takes my laptop. "You must always turn on VPN… and only go in virtual machine. Never forget." She does a few more clicks, then hands the device back to me. "Show me. May be fake."

I find the original chat area and the reply message and turn it towards Cho. "What do you think?"

She studies it, does a few more quick clicks and pauses, watching the screen. "Hard to say. This person fairly active, but could be cop, too."

"Good point. I know they're scouring these sites as well, looking for people to bust. How can I tell?"

"You can't. With encryption, no way to tell. You lurk first. Watch history."

"Oh." *And here I thought one post and I'll be on my way to exposing these scumbags.* "So, I guess I'll go down that hole and see what I can find."

"Be careful," Cho warns again.

"I *will*," I say, with a bit too much emphasis.

Why does everyone keep telling me that?

I go into the bedroom and spend a couple of hours going down the deep, black rabbit hole of the darknet, attempting to determine whether *lookforfun335* is a real trafficker, a scammer or a law enforcement officer. One link leads to another that leads to another and I'm taken in by the depravity of the conversations. I can only assume these are mostly men talking about their sexual interests, what they'd like to do with women and children, with some asking how they can sexually manipulate women. It turns my stomach, and I have to stop.

I stretch, and my neck is stiff from being in the same position for too long. Out the window the sun is in a slow descent over the ocean, casting orange and yellows and lavenders across the horizon. I realize I haven't walked to the beach yet.

Before I call the DHHS woman, I need to talk to Roger Lester at NCI. It takes him three rings to answer my call.

"TJ, how are ya? Sorry, I'm juggling a bunch of assignments here."

"No problem, I can call back."

"It's okay. How are you? Ready for another gig?"

"I'm good, but sorry, not yet. About to catch some sex traffickers. But I did want to ask you about a VP from NCI. Steven Godfrey, is it? Who is he?"

Rogers sighs. "I'm trying to figure him out, too. I meant to call you and give you a heads-up. Did you hear from him?"

"Yeah, he left a rambling message, about wanting to meet, something about a full-time position at NCI, and to cover another sting operation. You know anything about it?"

"Turns out he's the 'someone upstairs' who likes you and who landed you on the L.A. drug bust. He wondered if I had convinced you to work full-time for NCI, and he has an extortion operation he thought you'd do well on."

"What the hell, Rog? Who is this guy?"

"He's up there, TJ. He's head of the whole newsgathering division at NCI. He's got clout… and would probably be an advantageous person to have on your side."

"He sounds a little creepy to me. And where is he coming up with these assignments?"

"I agree. And I asked him the same thing. Says he can't reveal his 'sources.' But he's got good inside information."

"So, what do you think I should do, Roger?"

There's silence for a moment. "On one side, it couldn't hurt to meet him, and might be good for your career. On the other side, there's something about him… I'm not sure, I can't put my finger on it."

I mull this over. *Full-time? Would that mean based in one location? With a little place of my own? And an extortion case does sound interesting… Wait, there you go again: squirrel!*

"I'll give him a call. But please let me know if you hear anything else from him."

"Absolutely. Just… be careful, TJ."

"I've been hearing that a lot lately."

It's almost 5, but I put in another call to Kate O'Brien from the Department of Health and Human Services.

I'm pretty sure what she's going to say, but I want to document it anyway.

"This is Kate O'Brien."

No gatekeeper this time.

"Hi, Ms. O'Brien, this is TJ Banks calling again, regarding the migrant children sex-trafficking story I'm working on. We spoke a couple of days ago?"

"Yes?"

"So, I'm still trying to determine how such a thing could happen. Do you believe someone is working from inside the government to help these traffickers?"

"Ms. Banks, is it? Um, we don't have any evidence of that, but it is something we are looking into."

Ah-hah, I must be on the right track.

"Which department are you looking into?"

"Well, I certainly can't release that information—"

"But you must have some idea who they are. Is it Border Patrol? Or maybe ICE?"

"Ms. Banks, I cannot divulge any information on an ongoing invest—"

"And how many unethical people from the government are probably in on this? Two? Fifteen? More?"

"We have no idea how ma—"

"But you don't deny that there must be some internal corruption for this to take place?"

"No… I mean, we are not aware of—"

"Thanks, Ms. O'Brien. I'll be in touch."

I hang up on the sputtering government official and smile.

Chapter 51

Darkmover sits at a large, ornate desk, eyes glued to a large computer screen.

Long fingers glide across the keyboard. The monitor is the only light in the shadowy room. It's pitch black outside the tall windows.

A sequence of harsh knocks at the door.

"Come," Darkmover says, still focused on the computer display.

The wooden door opens and a man in a dark suit, white shirt and tie enters, solemn. He stands before his boss, hands rubbing together nervously.

"Yes?" Darkmover says impatiently, finally looking at the visitor.

"Vee may have trawble," the man says hesitantly.

"Vat ees eet dees time?" Darkmover goes back to the screen.

"Cineva este pe urmele noastre," he says in Romanian. Someone is on our trail.

This gets Darkmover's attention, who now swivels in the office chair to face the man. *"Oms?"* Who?

"Un reporter TV. Unul dintre spionii noștri dark web comunică cu ea." A TV reporter. One of our dark web spies is communicating with her.

"Reporter? TV?" Darkmover laughs. "Not to vorry. Eet ees not'ing." Darkmover turns back to the computer.

The man's upper lip is wet with perspiration, and he dries it off with a swipe of his hand. "She vork veeth FBI."

Darkmover looks up, the expression annoyed. "You haf name?"

The man pulls out a piece of paper from inside his suit coat and hands it to Darkmover, who studies it. "T'ank you. I handle." Darkmover dismisses the man with a nod toward the door. The man bows his head and hurries out.

Darkmover studies the paper, then rips it into small pieces, and tosses it in the trash. Leaning back in the chair, fingertips steepled together, tapping, the Romanian trafficker contemplates the next move.

Chapter 52

It's hard to tell the sun is up in Los Angeles, as it's a typical gray and smoggy morning on the West Coast.

Cho and I hug goodbye at her door, and my bag is in the rental car. After being cooped up inside for most of my stay with my cyber friend, I want to get a few minutes at the water before I leave.

I stride quickly across the boardwalk to the Venice Beach surf, where there's a chilly trade wind. I tug my jacket closed. Except for a colony of sea gulls looking for food, I'm one of the few on the sand at this early hour. A couple of joggers sprint by, and a vehicle sweeps the shore for litter, leaving long tire lines in a repeating pattern in the sand.

The sea is mesmerizing as the roaring waves wash in and then quietly slip out. *I do love the ocean. There's something so calming, satisfying, about it.* The repetition, the sound, the changing swirls, all lull my body into a relaxed state, something I don't experience often.

But I also need sunshine. Maybe the trip to Phoenix will help me weigh in on the debate of whether to get my own place or not. *Then there's New Mexico, which is a lot like Arizona, and Aaron is there…*

I shake my head. "Eye on the prize, Banks." *Keep your head in the game and don't get distracted.* I'm after sex traffickers, and those who sell children are the ultimate scum of the earth. Snippets of the darknet chats ping my brain: *"…want to do a little girl, no boobs yet…" "just let me get an 8yo boy off!"*

I feel bile rise in my throat. *They must be stopped. No matter what.*

I trudge through the sand back to the car.

Next stop: Phoenix.

It's a sweet ride in the shiny Porsche from the car rental facility to the Federal Bureau of Investigation's Phoenix Division building on the far north side of the Valley, where I'll meet with Agent Toni Karls.

While I drive north on I-17, the 65-mph speed limit doesn't begin to show what the Porsche can really do. *Maybe I'll take it out on the freeway in the next couple of days. Drive up to Sedona and see what this vehicle can do.* Yeah, I'll head "up the hill" as Michael referred to it. *Jeez, will you quit obsessing about him!*

As I pull into the driveway, I'm greeted by a large metal and stone sign marked with an enormous thumbprint and "FBI." As I get closer to the building, I see that a couple dozen skinny rectangular windows in turquoise blue are spaced out along the long exterior. According to a local article I read, written when the structure was built about a dozen years ago, the shape of the glass was intended to look like DNA markers.

The fingerprint theme continues in the landscape design of stacked rocks and bushes in long circular shapes outside the front door. Inside the heavily secured structure, more prints and DNA markers decorate the lobby, the tile floors and the carpet.

I successfully pass through a metal detector and am given a visitor's badge, yes, with another spiraling whorl on it. *Wonder if it's someone's real fingerprint?*

A gruff-looking man in the stereotypical dark blue suit, white shirt and tie with a clear wire curling out of his left ear points me toward the elevators and the fourth floor.

Chapter 53

Agent Karls finally comes to the door of the reception area around about 10:20 a.m.

"Ms. Banks."

Curt. All business. She's smaller than I thought she would be, and her glum face is surrounded by short mousy brown curls. Her tailored suit and pants say "no nonsense" as do her flat rubber-soled shoes.

She doesn't offer to shake my hand, and merely gestures with her left towards the wide hallway. She walks silently beside me, then turns right. The door is marked "KARLS" with another tall blue DNA marker glass on the side.

It's a small interior office, no outside windows, and she takes a seat behind her government issue desk and clasps her hands in front of her. I sit in one of the two chairs on the other side and pull out my iPad to refer to my research and take notes.

"Thanks for seeing me today, Agent Karls."

"Agent Porter put in a good word for you, but my time is limited. What kind of information do you think you have?"

She's going to be a tough one. Sugar, not vinegar, TJ.

"We are confident that we have the address of a probable sex-trafficking house holding migrant children here." Karls's face is blank. I continue. "In addition, we believe there are multiple people working inside the government to move young boys and girls who are separated from their parents at the border into a handful of so-called 'foster homes.'" I pause, glancing at my tablet. "I've talked to both Kate O'Brien from DHHS and a Cooper Miller from Homeland Security. Ms. O'Brien confirmed they were looking into the government corruption angle, but neither would explain how this could possibly happen. Could you?"

Karls continues to stare at me but flexes her fingers as if stalling for time.

"Ms. Banks, the Department of Health and Human Services has strong policies in place to ensure the privacy and safety of unaccompanied children. HHS works with state officials to address concerns they may have about the care of or impact on unaccompanied children in their states, while making sure the children are treated humanely and consistent with the law as they go through immigration court proceedings."

I bite my tongue as she spews the company line.

She continues. "When a child who is not accompanied by a parent or legal guardian is apprehended by immigration authorities, the child is transferred to the care and custody of the Office of Refugee Resettlement."

There's a division I'm not familiar with. I type in that name as Karls resumes what sounds like a rehearsed and oft repeated script.

"Federal law requires that ORR feed, shelter and provide medical care for unaccompanied children until it is able to release them to safe settings with sponsors while they await immigration proceedings. These sponsors, usually family members, live in many states and all must pass background checks. The sponsor must agree—"

"I understand how it's supposed to work," I interrupt. "But Agent Porter found a house in New York—"

"Which was a terrible oversight and we are rectifying—"

I feel my face flush. "Oversight? But those children have not been found, have they?"

Karls' jaw clenches as she stares at me, stony-faced. I wait.

"We are doing everything in our power to find them, Ms. Banks. Now, if you have additional information that would aid in our efforts, we would appreciate you doing your civic duty to turn it over."

Civic duty, my ass. "Does the name 'Darkmover' mean anything to you?"

Chapter 54

Karls blinks a couple of times and looks down, as if searching her memory banks.

Her chocolate-colored eyes meet mine again. "Not off the top of my head, why?"

"We believe this is a major sex trafficker in Europe, and that one or more of your corrupt government officials are working with him to move the migrant kids."

A dark look flashes briefly through her eyes, until Karls looks down to jot the name on a pad in front of her. "I will certainly investigate it." Her voice is frosty. "What else?"

"We are still trying to track down the exact government department involved, but our research on the deep web has revealed an address of a home in South Phoenix that is believed to be holding a number of boys and girls."

Karls is poised to write again. "Go ahead…"

I smile. "Not so fast. You must agree to let me be in on the bust with my video camera. I will—"

"Ms. Banks, that is absolutely not going to happen. We have strict—"

"As I was saying, I will take complete responsibility for my welfare, and will sign any agreement relieving you of any liability. This is a story that the public needs to know about, and it could go far in helping to shut down the other houses if these scumbags are aware the FBI is on to them."

The agent thinks for a moment. "*If* you were allowed to go, it absolutely cannot be live. In case—"

"Agreed. Videotaped only, not live." *Yes!* "This could be quite a feather in your cap if it is successful."

"I'm not in this for the credit, Ms. Banks."

"But you can't deny being interviewed on national television as the one who organized this takedown wouldn't raise your profile within the department. And a letter of recommendation in your file can't hurt."

Karls's jaw clenches back and forth, and her eyes narrow.

Shit, is she going to say no?

Then she dips her head, realizing. "We have much work to do—"

"And every second counts. Something we can both agree on." I pull out small card with the address written and hand it to the agent. "Okay, here's what I suggest…"

A plan in place, Karls gives her assurance she will contact me as soon as everything and everyone is ready. Of course, that's not to say she won't just go ahead and do the bust on her own… but I think the lure of her potential televised achievement is in the back of her mind.

When I get to my car in the FBI parking lot, I call Aaron Porter. I can't wait to break the news.

He answers on the first ring. "Banks?"

"Ahh, I must be in your contacts now. Movin' up in the world," I jest.

"Whatcha need, Banks?"

"And we're back to business. Okay, just had a productive meeting with Agent Karls here in Phoenix and we are a go for the bust. Not sure exactly—"

"Yes, I know, Banks. Karls told me. I'm on my way out there."

I don't allow myself to get caught by surprise very often, so this is a rare moment. "Uh, really, that was fast. And great." My heart beats just a little faster and I get that warm feeling in my stomach to think of him being here in Phoenix.

Porter continues. "I'm heading to the airport in a few minutes, and with the time zone difference, should be in by dinner."

I pause for a beat. "Is… that an invitation?"

Silence. Then, "If you like."

Another beat. I smile. "I like. I'll pick you up at Sky Harbor. Porter, I just hope you can squeeze into a Porsche."

Chapter 55

Aaron folds his 6'4" frame into the small foreign car, then he and I end up grabbing drive-through burgers on our way to a meeting at Phoenix Police Department headquarters downtown.

Hopefully there will be time for a nice quiet dinner together later...

The South Phoenix house in question has been under surveillance since I gave Agent Karls the address. Officers report not seeing much activity and question whether migrant children are being held there for sex purposes or whether the adult occupants can tell they are being watched.

"Judge Martin is sympathetic to the cause," says Maricopa County Assistant District Attorney Sheila Roe. "But he's mulling over whether he can take the word of dark web hackers to sign the warrants we need."

I can feel my face turning a shade of pink with embarrassment. This operation is mostly based on information I brought to them, which even I will admit may be questionable... and potentially inaccurate. But I shake it off. "Think of the children. If it's not what you think it is, you apologize. But if it is, you've got to get the kids out."

Roe considers this, and gives a slight nod, her graying bob swaying around her face. "He's good with the search and seizure warrant, but it's the no-knock entry he's debating. There have been some high-profile incidents where no-knock warrants have led to bloodshed and loss of life."

Aaron counters. "If there are traffickers, there's no doubt of reasonable suspicion of officer danger. Of course, the kids could get caught in the middle as well."

Roe continues. "And don't forget occupants can use deadly force, and in combination with the no-knock warrant, it can lead to tragic outcomes for both law enforcement and civilians."

There's silence for a moment.

"Did you tell the judge we could also be closer to finding out who in the government may be funneling these kids to traffickers?" I ask.

"He's fully aware," Roe says, her tone reflecting the authority of her office.

Aaron takes the lead. "While we wait, let's go over the operation one more time."

Search and seizure as well as the no-knock warrants are in hand, thanks to Aaron's call, convincing the judge.

We're scheduled for another middle-of-the-night operation, this time at 4 a.m. Phoenix P.D.'s SWAT team will go in first with the FBI right behind. I will follow Aaron and Agent Karls with my camera.

Phoenix officers, including the SWAT team, all wear body-worn cameras. In addition, the cops in the lead carry head-to-knee bulletproof shields for protection, anticipating the worst. Ballistic helmets, the kind used in riots or ambushes, are passed out to everyone. While they're mostly rated for handgun bullets, they have been known to save the lives of officers hit with rifles and other weapons, mostly because of the deflecting properties of the contoured shape and bulletproof material.

The helmet keeps me from looking directly into the camera's eyepiece. I'm able to add a small monitor so I can see the action I'll be taping. *Ready.*

I have strict orders from Aaron to stay outside the house in question, and he assures me that I will be given access to portions of the body-worn camera footage for my report. My argument that I still managed to get a bullet wound being *outside* the L.A. drug bust didn't sway him in the least. While I always want to be where the main action is, I continue to feel twinges of pain in my healing calf from that experience, and I hide my relief that I won't be going into the building.

A command post is set up a couple of blocks away, where the Phoenix Fire Department paramedics, social workers and other DHHS personnel wait.

The unsettling feeling of déjà vu hits me once again as my camera records the law enforcement group as they storm the house and use a battering ram to break down the front door.

"Police!" "FBI!" "Hands up!"

Chapter 56

From my vantage point behind a tall mesquite tree—also for potential "protection," according to Aaron, although I debate whether the skinny trunk will do much good—the entire two-story, pink stucco house is in my camera's view.

Officers shout "Clear!" as they go through the rooms. *Wait a minute, it sounds like there are too many cleared or empty rooms. That is not a good sign! I should hear other voices by now. Shouldn't they be finding someone? Anyone? Sleeping children or adults? Did the traffickers get word and move everyone out—again?*

My attention is drawn to a light tapping on glass. I keep the camera pointed at the front door, but look around, not seeing anything. More tapping, urgent. I look around cautiously and run over to the left side of the building where thick purple ruellia bushes surround the tall house. I look up at the windows above, but that's not where the sound is coming from. It seems to be emanating from behind the plants. I push my camera lens through the green leaves and purple flowers—and the anguished face of a small child fills my lens, startling me.

Shocked, I pull the camera away and separate the four-foot-tall branches again with my left arm—and see the same little one, maybe a girl, tears running down her face, beating on a below-ground window now with her grimy palms, her wrists zip-tied together.

"Aaron! Someone! Help me!" I shout, but am not sure anyone can hear.

I toss down my camera onto the ground and use both hands to push aside the bushes. The small rectangular window is heavily caulked all around, and I peer into what seems to be a basement. The pounding continues, and even in the darkness, I can see other children inside, terrified, huddled on dirty mattresses or on the bare cement floor.

"Oh my god! I'll get you out!" I frantically look for a rock, anything to break the window. Finding nothing, I pick up my camera and wonder how strong the square back of the metal housing is. *Use the whole damn thing if you need. You can buy another one.*

I gesture to the little girl in a shooing motion and say, "Move back, honey." She takes a couple of steps away and I smash the back end of the camera through the glass, sending shards into the room.

Soft little hands reach to me through the opening, and I grab them, gently pulling up the child, hoping she doesn't get cut by the broken slivers. Other kids line up behind her and—

"Stop right there." A deep male voice murmurs loudly, so close to my left ear I can feel the man's stale, hot breath. I freeze, the little girl half in, half out of the basement. "Put her down. Now!"

Chapter 57

I don't let go.

I *won't* let go.

I glance to the side and there's a large silver gun pointed directly at me, inches from my face. I gasp in fear, and at the end of the man's arm a large stocking-masked head comes into view.

"Put her down now, or I shoot!"

"She's just a baby!" Hot angry tears threaten to fall as I clutch the little girl and her bound and grimy hands cling to me so tightly, her long, thin fingernails boring into my skin. "What if she were your daughter? Or your niece? You know this isn't ri—"

The gun suddenly swings away from me, and at the same time there's a loud, dull *thud* as the man goes down on the ground. Behind him, Agent Aaron Porter stands with the metal battering ram in his hands, now bloodied after striking the sex trafficker.

"Thank god!" I smile, as I carefully pull the child out through the window. She curls into my arms, and she's crying, and despite the smells of urine and grime and greasy hair, I hold her close and keep repeating, "You're okay now, honey, you're going to be just fine."

No one expected to find a basement, as they are rare in Arizona homes, due to the high cost and hard desert ground.

In addition, the ground-floor entrance stairs down to the level below was blocked and totally invisible from the inside.

Aaron and the others were perplexed not to find anyone on the first or second floors. But after the seven children were discovered through the small lower window outside, they also found the hidden entrance inside, cleverly concealed by a bookshelf on wheels.

Only one young man in his 20s was stationed in the basement overnight to watch the kids—five girls and two boys, ranging in age from 8 to 12—and he was fast asleep until the glass broke. He admitted to police that the rest of the traffickers were in the house next door, and guessed that all but the one who accosted me had heard the police presence and managed to escape. I watch him taken away in an ambulance, police following.

Before finally relinquishing my tight hold on the child, I'm surprised at the new images flashing through my brain of me reading to her, bathing her, dressing her. I've never really considered having a child, but a strong maternal instinct overwhelms me, if briefly.

I reluctantly let the youngster go when a social worker and a female Phoenix police officer arrive, assuring me multiple times they will take good care of her.

I don't think I'll ever forget the sweet look on the little girl's face as she gives me a kiss on my cheek. Then she's gone, and my arms feel empty.

Aaron has shot dark looks my way since bashing the man's head, but in the hubbub, we haven't had a chance to speak.

My camera is banged up but basically operational, and I'm excited to see that it's still recording. While the video is of the bushes in a static shot on its side, it catches all the sounds of the glass breaking, the child's sobs, the trafficker's voice, Aaron's blow to the man's head and the rescue of the little girl.

Still a little shaky, I convince Agent Toni Karls to do an interview on site. Through the camera's cracked monitor, her hair a little wild after removing her helmet, Karls is the epitome of the Bureau's composure and calm.

"Today the Federal Bureau of Investigation, along with the Phoenix Police Department, rescued seven migrant children under the age of 12 from a suspected sex-trafficking house in Phoenix, Arizona. The children were being restrained in the basement of the house with one guard, who was arrested and is being held pending charges of kidnapping, child sex trafficking, sexual exploitation of a minor and prostitution. A second suspect was injured and sent to the hospital and will face the same charges along with assault with a deadly weapon.

"We appreciate the partnership of local law enforcement and media who assisted in shutting this house down. We will be working diligently to place these children back with their parents."

I smile at her reference to me as "media" who helped. "What do you say to people who may live next door to such a heinous crime taking place?"

"We urge residents that if they see something, to say something, no matter how insignificant they believe it might be. Adults coming and going from a house at all times of the day or night, hearing children but never seeing them, may point toward something monstrous like this going on. Please, call your local police department and make a report if something doesn't look quite right."

"Agent Karls, these children were separated from their parents by the government when they crossed the border into the United States. They were supposed to have been placed in foster homes until the legal process was complete. How could they have been placed directly into the hands of sex traffickers?"

"The Department of Health and Human Services has strong policies in place to ensure—"

She stops. She knows this is not necessarily the case anymore. "Obviously there has been a severe breach in our protocols to protect these children. We will do everything in our power to bring these monsters to justice."

"And if there is corruption within the government that enabled this?"

"While we have no evidence that is the case as of yet, again, we will do everything we can to find everyone who may be part of this and make sure they face the harshest penalty of the law. That's all I have."

With that, Karls turns and strides briskly toward the command post.

Chapter 58

As the sun rises over the crime scene, people in the neighborhood, many still in robes, chat in small group conversations, concerned looks on their faces.

Paramedics tend to the children, who are mostly dehydrated and hungry with only minor wounds from the broken glass. SWAT and Phoenix PD officers remove, clean and put away their gear. Patrol officers go door to door to interview residents to find out what they know about the traffickers.

I have more than enough footage needed for a great story.

Agent Porter comes out of the command post and stomps toward me.

I take a few steps his way. "Thanks so much, Aaron, your timing was perfect. Hey, I'm starving. Wanna go for break—"

"Banks, what the fuck were you thinking?" His eyes are coal black, and I've never seen anger like this on his face.

"Wha—?" I start, but he interrupts again.

"You never follow orders. You can't stay in one place. You put yourself and others at risk—"

"Hold on a minute, Porter." Now I'm pissed. "I heard a tapping noise coming from the basement, and I went to see what it was. If you recall, I'm the one who—"

"Once again, it's all about you. *You* have to get the footage. *You* have to horn your way into operations that are dangerous enough without us having to babysit a civilian. *You*—"

"Babysit?!" My hands clench. "Are you shitting me? I—"

"Let me finish!" he roars. "You caught a bullet in your leg last time. Today you almost had your head blown off. You are media. You are supposed to be *covering* the news, not making the news."

I squeeze my jaws together and don't respond. We glare at each other. For a brief moment I want to stroke his beautiful ebony cheek, and in the next moment, I want to punch it.

"I had to help that little girl," I say quietly. "I wasn't going to just keep videotaping and wait until someone finally came out."

"Law enforcement, paramedics, all of *us* have the job of helping people. I thought you reporters are trained to 'bear witness.'"

"Yes, I have a job to do, and that usually means being an impartial observer. But in a case of imminent danger—"

"You almost got yourself killed!" His face pushes in front of mine, and as his voice booms, I can smell the mints on his breath.

"I'm a human being, too!" I scream.

It's suddenly quiet around us, and as I glance around, people try not to look at us.

I lower my voice. "Obviously, this is an issue on which we don't agree. I have a report to file." I turn quickly and stride down the street.

That's when I realize I rode here with Aaron and others in a Phoenix PD van.

Damn.

I pull out my cell phone and call an Uber.

Chapter 59

Steven Godfrey's cell phone rings as he sits down to dinner with his wife, Linda, in the opulent dining room of their red-brick Georgetown home.

His brows furrow, as he doesn't recognize the number on his screen, and there's no caller ID associated with it.

"Sorry, honey, I'd better take this."

Godfrey gets up from the table and goes into his den.

"Hello?"

An angry nasal voice chastises him. "Godfrey, I thought I told you to rein in that pit bull of a reporter unless she was working on *our* projects."

"Charlie, is that you?" Godfrey forces a laugh. "Sorry, I didn't recognize the number. Ha, you must be calling on a burner phone or something."

There is silence on the line until the man on the other end says, "Well?"

"Oh. Yeah. Now, you know that TJ Banks is a freelancer, so I don't have a lot of control over what she does." He takes a deep breath. "She did a helluva job on that sting operation in L.A., didn't she?"

"That's beside the point. What's her obsession with those damned stories about migrants and whores? You've got to distract her from them, and keep her on our jobs."

Godfrey's voice chokes. "Well, uh, I'll see what I can—"

"You'd better do more than that. Keep in mind the government has many resources to take care of things like this."

"Wait a minute, what do you mean?" Godfrey feels a flash of heat on his forehead and nervously loosens his tie.

"And we also have many restrictions we can put in place that would cripple your organization. Don't make me do that, Godfrey."

"I'll talk to her, Charlie. Not to worry."

But by the frown on Steven Godfrey's face, it's obvious he's very worried.

Who the hell is this guy really?! And what "restrictions" is he talking about?

Chapter 60

I spend the rest of the morning editing different versions of the raid, and since I got such an early start, it's barely noon.

I give first rights of my footage to Always Online Digital News, then sell various packages and footage to CNN, NCI and MSNBC.

I don't open Aaron's five texts. Or his three emails. Or his two voice messages. The footage from the raid goes directly to Agent Karls.

I should take a nap, but my mind swirls with images of the adorable little girl at the sting and with Aaron's harsh words.

Time for that road trip in the rental sports car.

It's an extra sweet ride in the Porsche convertible on my way to Sedona.

A balmy 76 degrees with the top down, I've got nothing but beautiful blue skies and plenty of sunshine to soak in. Not like the smog and gray mornings in Los Angeles. *Hmm, maybe Phoenix might be a decent place to live.* I've heard about the hot summers, but otherwise the weather is gorgeous most of the time.

Wait a minute, Michael is here. My former fiancé. A big shot TV anchor now. Married, soon to be father. Right. That wouldn't be good. In fact, it would be too hard for me living in his own backyard. *Scratch off Arizona. You've gotta stop thinking about that guy. He's certainly stopped thinking about you.*

Aaron's angry face, yelling at me this morning, flashes in my brain. I thought we might have something together…

Stop. Get Aaron out of your head, too. He showed his true colors this morning. Concentrate on the drive.

With the air whipping through my short hair, I clear my head by cranking a playlist of women rock 'n roll musicians. The Porsche takes my mind off everything and doesn't disappoint. On the straightaways well outside the Phoenix city limits, the little powerhouse easily surges up to 115 mph—too easily perhaps—and the rush of the wind around my face and head and ears is exhilarating. The changing landscape of saguaro cactus to scrub trees and wildflowers is mostly a blur, and I feel like a race car driver. The vehicle hugs the asphalt up the hills and around the curves, leaving me snug and comfortable in the tight seatbelt.

I grin like a crazy hyena despite the looks of disdain from fellow freeway drivers as I zip past them. The vehicles on the road look like they are parked as I whiz around them.

I have my fun and a huge helping of good luck, with no cops to ticket me, so I get off the highway at exit 287 to have a late lunch in the little town of Cottonwood. I salivate at the thought of an Italian lunch at Nic's, which was recommended by the hotel concierge. Then I'll drive on to Sedona, maybe do some hiking in the red rocks, find the best restaurant to watch the sunset during dinner and spend the night at a swanky resort hotel. Sleep in and drive back to Phoenix in the morning.

My cell dings with yet another text message from Steven Godfrey, the VP from NCI. Since 7 this morning, my cell is filled with multiple annoying voicemails from him, all gushing about my work, my footage, my stories, and what an "asset" I'd be to them if I worked for NCI exclusively. Stuff like that is usually nice to hear, and as a freelancer, this kind of thing is rare. My paycheck is usually my praise.

But I guess it's the cynicism in me that makes me wary of this guy and his schmaltzy compliments. He is certainly persistent, doesn't want to talk over the phone, and insists we meet in person. He says he will fly out on the company's private corporate jet to wherever I am.

I give in and agree to meet him in Sedona. I tell him I'll text the restaurant name when I have it.

Chapter 61

Lucky me.

It's $5-off-any-appetizer day at Nic's, so I order the Crabby Mac-n-Cheese. The Alfredo sauce is bubbling hot and the generous portion of real lump crabmeat is sweet and tasty.

So, surf-and-turf is a little hokey, but my mouth waters again. I go for the ribeye, which promises to be grilled Tuscan style with "just the right seasonings," along with a market-price lobster. I don't ask how much it is, nor do I really want to know where it comes from before it landed here in the desert. If the photos tell half the story, it will be delicious.

I think about Roger, in his condo in Atlanta, and what a foodie he is. He would love this meal, and with all the restaurants around him, probably takes time to enjoy them much than I do. *Maybe I need to think more seriously about him.* We do get along great. But does he have deeper feelings for me than I do for him? That could be a problem.

I'm stuffed.

A strong cappuccino dilutes the alcohol in the red wine I had with lunch. Just to be on the safe side, I take a stroll down the street, do some window shopping, get a tall to-go cup of hot coffee and enjoy the beautiful sunshine before getting back in the car to drive on to Sedona.

I take highway 89A out of Cottonwood, which locals consider a "back road" but is still two lanes in each direction. It's mostly a flat, straight shot through dry desert until outcroppings of rocks start to appear.

And there are those striking, beautiful red rocks in the distance.

I realize it's been years since I've been to Sedona, and it was also my "treat" after covering a story in Scottsdale in my early days of freelancing. The house of the Sadowski family had burned down, and investigators eventually found the charred remains of three of the four family members: those of the wife and two children. Turns out they had all been shot, and the husband and father, Joseph Sadowski, was the suspect. He was eventually found and thrown in prison for three lifetimes.

I think about how green I was during that time and remember throwing up for the first—and last—time at a traumatic incident scene.

Initially, I couldn't discern what I was smelling while videotaping the smoke and ash after the fire was contained. It was a weird combination of sweet and putrid and copper and rotten eggs.

A Scottsdale firefighter later explained a burnt body is different from cooked meat from a butcher. Grilled steaks are mostly free of blood, where human flesh is full of it. When it "cooks," there's a coppery tinge to the aroma.

He told me internal organs literally boil in all the water they contain, and it produces a liver-like stink. Spinal fluid burns up in a musky, sweet perfume.

Then there's the sulfur odor of burnt hair, which took days to get out of my nose.

Put them all together, and I couldn't help but hurl. A police officer approached me, and at first, I thought he was there to help. Turns out he just gave me a trash bag to vomit into so I wouldn't mess up his crime scene.

If Sedona wasn't so far from Phoenix Sky Harbor airport…

My reverie is broken when a large black SUV zooms up behind me. I ease off the accelerator a bit, thinking he wants to pass. But he slows down and comes within inches of my back bumper.

What the…?

Chapter 62

W_ho is this guy and what is he doing?_
Time to let the Porsche show its stuff again. I floor the gas pedal and the blue beauty takes off in a flash and climbs to an easy 100 mph. I figure it's just some jerk who is jealous of my ride and—

But the SUV is back. And it's even closer. Both the driver and passenger wear dark sunglasses. And is that a weapon coming out of the window, pointing at me?

I start a serpentine path, turning one way and the other, and increase my speed even more, wary of a few other drivers on the road. The SUV stays on my tail. There's a loud pop and the sound of probably a bullet whizzing by my left ear.

"Fuck! Siri, call 9-1-1!" I shout to my phone. When I hear "Where is your emergency?" in my earpiece, I frantically try to see a mile marker, but can't. "I'm somewhere on 89A coming into Sedona! I have someone on my tail shooting at me!"

"That would be Yavapai County. Transferring you now." The dispatcher is way too calm. _Did she not hear me??_

"Siri, navigate to Sedona Police headquarters!"

"Getting directions to Sedona Police Department," my phone states. Another damned composed voice.

By now I'm racing closer to town, and zip by a "Red Rock State Park" sign. My sweaty hands clutch the steering wheel.

"Continue on 89A for one-and-a-half miles."

When Yavapai County emergency services comes on the line, it's yet another unruffled dispatcher. I try to stay as calm as I can, but even I can hear the panic in my voice. "I passed the turnoff for the Red Rock Park about a minute ago… and I see a sign for a Marriott ahead."

"That would be Sedona Police. I'll transfer you."

"Are you kidding me?!" but she's gone and all I hear is wind rushing past me and the squeals of the driver behind me trying to match my traversing.

"In half a mile, turn left on Roadrunner Drive," says my phone's navigation voice.

"Sedona Police, Lieutenant Harvey." This one sounds bored.

"I need help. I'm in a vehicle and I'm being chased by a black SUV and shot at! On 89A coming into Sedona. I think I just passed a high school… and we're both driving at high speed."

Another pop, pop and the passenger-side mirror glass explodes.

"Shit! He just shot my car!"

"Ma'am, we've got officers enroute. I have your location, and I'll direct you to the Sedona Police Department. You'll see the Mystical Bazaar gift shop on your left, and that's where you'll turn left onto Roadrunner Drive."

"Pass the Mystical Bazaar gift shop, then turn left," repeats my phone.

Sirens wail from both directions. I'm in town now, and swerve around traffic, hoping like hell I won't hit someone or the shooter won't shoot someone. Especially not me. I'm still doing 65 in the busy four lanes of traffic.

"Take the next left."

At the last second, I slam on the brakes and fishtail a couple of times before straightening out on Roadrunner Drive. The SUV blows past the intersection.

"Ma'am, take a right on the second driveway—"

"Too late, I've missed it."

"Then the next right is Cardinal Lane. Follow it around to the back."

I see "Cardinal Lane" flash by, and I turn the steering wheel and punch the brakes just hard enough to spin me around back to the street. I speed around the corner and fly by a sign for "Sedona School of Massage." *I'm going to need one after this.*

Police officers in blue uniforms frantically wave their arms at me as I peel into the parking lot and come to a stop.

Talk about an adrenaline shot. I'm breathing hard and sweating and my heart is hammering in my chest.

But there's no sign of the SUV.

I'm safe. For now.

But who the hell was that?

Chapter 63

By the time police reports are filed and insurance forms started for the damage on the rental car, it's late afternoon.

No sign of the SUV that was chasing me. A couple of traffic cams pick it up but can't get a license plate before it goes into the wind.

The post-adrenaline fatigue settling into my bones makes me question whether I should have that sunset dinner I promised myself or just drive back to the Valley now. But I need to eat, and I'll be damned if I'm going to let this episode deter me from enjoying a meal.

I let a Sedona police officer escort me to Enchantment, a beautiful resort at the base of the red rocks in Boynton Canyon, and don't argue with him when he says he'll stay on property until I leave.

In one breath, I want to call Aaron to tell him about the last few hours. In the next breath, I want to push him out of my brain. He's just going to yell at me anyway.

And I now regret agreeing to meet Steven Godfrey here. The guy hopped right on NCI's private jet earlier this afternoon and has been pinging me for my location from the Sedona airport. But I send him a quick text telling him *not* to come until after I eat.

I get a window table in the restaurant and blow out a breath as I finally relax with a glass of Scotch. Surrounded by the dipping sun over the incredible red rocks, it's peaceful and so serene here. Much needed after the past 48 hours of the sting op and being chased and shot at and almost run off the road.

Speaking of which. Maybe it's time to come *off the road.* I feel a weariness, a heavy weight that is new. Maybe that's the pressure of the freelance world. Never knowing where your next job is coming from or where it's going to take you. I don't have as much "feast or famine" as I did early in my career, and I am lucky to stay very busy, but who knows?

That, too, could change with younger, faster, cheaper reporters in competition with me.

Maybe that's it. At 39, am I getting too old for this business? Most of the time I still feel as if I'm 25, but recovering from the bullet wound, along with the dangers I've been putting myself in, and I'm feeling all my years, plus some.

Albuquerque is out. Obviously, Aaron and I just don't have enough in common. Sure, the sex is great, but it would be nice to have a partner who is also a solid friend, too.

I could probably get a place in Atlanta, where I'd know Roger. He's a sweet guy, and it's no secret he's always had a thing for me. We've been good friends for a long time. Maybe that could lead to something else, if I let it.

I've kept so many people at arm's length for so long, there aren't too many friends in my life, male or female. And that disappoints and saddens me. Maybe with a saner schedule, and my own place where I could actually entertain people, I'd also make some new friends along the way. Maybe there'd be more time to look for Katrina and get a do-over with her.

And that little girl. *Do I feel the faint ticking of a biological clock?*

That's new.

And, in one of his messages, the $300,000 salary Godfrey tossed out like it was chump change did get my attention.

After dinner, I wait for the NCI VP in the bar off the lobby of the resort.

Chapter 64

"TJ! Steven Godfrey. How are ya?" A booming voice shatters my reverie.

A large man with a gut pushing out his yellow polo shirt strides toward my table. I stand to greet him, hand out, and I can tell my forced smile is a weak one.

"Oh, let me give you a hug," he chortles, and grabs me way too tight, for way too long.

I manage to break away and take my chair again. "Nice to meet you, Mr. Godfrey."

"No, no, please, you gotta call me Steve. This is not a corporate thing."

It's not? Then what is it? Now I'm more worried.

"Give me a margarita on the rocks with lots of salt," he shouts to the bartender. He turns back to me and chuckles. "When in Rome…" He casually leans back in his chair and finally lowers his voice. "I hear you've had a helluva couple of days, what with that sex trafficking thing."

"Not to mention being chased and shot at today," I add.

He gulps, and his whole body language changes. He leans his arms on the table, hands folded together but twisting in and out. His face is red and it looks like he might throw up. *What the hell?*

"About that. I'm… so sorry that happened. I…" He takes a big breath and slips back into his brash self. "Now, if you came into our NCI fold, you wouldn't have to worry about crap like that, we'd take good care of you. You would have your pick of assignments that would bring you some real notoriety and lots of awards. You can have your own staff, an assistant, access to all the technology we have, which is impressive. Whatever you want, it will be at your disposal. Whaddaya say, TJ?"

Wow, at my disposal? Better tech? An assistant to make flight and hotel arrangements? Plum jobs I choose rather than whatever pops up next?

"About assignments. I have been very interested in doing what I can to bring sex traffickers to justice. Would I be able to continue that work?"

Anxiety hits his face again, with pursed lips and another gulp. "We can certainly… uh, talk about that." He puts one of his hands over mine, and the creepy Veep is back. "I see big things ahead for you."

I nonchalantly pull my hand back to take a sip of my drink. "It sounds very… interesting, Mr., er, Steve."

"And you tell me where you want to be located. I'm in Washington, D.C., of course, and it's a hot place for pros like you. Or there's Atlanta, New York or Los Angeles. Wherever you want to go." He takes a big gulp of his margarita. "I'll even throw in a luxury apartment like Roger's. Of course, you can pick it out. You could start, say, next week?"

"Whoa, hold on. You're moving a little too fast." *Something doesn't pass the smell test here.* "Why me? Why now?"

"What, are you kidding? You're a rising star! I've been watching you for some time now, and I've always been impressed. Roger speaks very highly of you, too. We need more hard-working go-getters like you at NCI. C'mon, TJ. It's time to move up to the next level."

The old "too good to be true" adage screams in my head, but most of it appears flipping amazing. "Look, it sounds… wonderful. But it's a big change, and I gotta think about it."

"Sure, sure, of course you do. Look, let's meet for breakfast tomorrow and we can discuss it more, answer any questions you might have." He finishes his drink in several successive swallows. "I'm gonna hit the hot tub. See ya mañana."

He tosses a $50 bill on the table and stumbles a bit as he leaves the bar.

I blink a couple of times in amazement. *Now what am I going to do?*

First decision: I'm not spending the night, although Enchantment is a beautiful resort.

Second decision: I'm not meeting with Godfrey in the morning.

My adrenaline boosted by this strange encounter with the news exec, I hop back in the car. The stars glitter above me, bright and amazing, as I head out of Boynton Canyon, flanked by a couple of Sedona police officers. At the edge of the city limits, Yavapai County Sheriff's deputies take over my escort. Once I'm on the freeway back to Phoenix, I put the Porsche top up, as temperatures have dipped. The deputies hand me off to Maricopa County authorities at the Black Canyon City exit, in the parking lot in front of a pie restaurant. The two vehicles, one in front, one in back, escort me directly to the rental car terminal. Then one deputy, a thin guy named Hollander, drops me at Sky Harbor's Southwest departure terminal. I convince him he does not need to accompany me inside, that I'll be safe at the airport with lots of people around.

Next stop: Atlanta. To see Roger. Talk about NCI. And my life.

Chapter 65

Aaron Porter spends the next few hours debriefing with the FBI team and Phoenix PD.

Beneath his professional outward demeanor, he seethes inside about TJ Banks. How she could've been killed. How reckless she was. How she put herself and others in danger. Yes, she found the children, but things could've gone terribly wrong.

I can't deal with her anymore. He rubs his hands over his face. *There are many things that attract me to her, but too many others that scare the shit outta me.* Her sentence on the phone the other day when she said, "If I didn't know any better, I'd think you might actually care" reverberates in his head. *I do, but I can't. Not any longer. Gotta find someone safer, more dependable. Gotta get TJ outta my head.*

He interviews the young trafficker caught in the migrant house. He's Jared Jordon, 22, from Glendale, Arizona, who doesn't seem to have much concrete information about the people he was working with. Except for the initials "BS," he knows little about the leader or leaders of the operation, where they came from, or where they might set up next. He gives up a few first names, but "Chan," "Stormer," "Tails" and "BS" all are most certainly nicknames.

Porter can smell the fear emanating from the pimply-faced kid, his long stringy hair hanging over his eyes.

One curious thing the young man did say was that his cohorts would joke about the main man they got instructions from, saying he was "more *orrr* less"—emphasizing and elongating the "or"—a puppet for someone else, then they'd laugh. The kid didn't seem to understand what it meant, and neither did Porter.

He pops a cinnamon mint into his mouth.

Chapter 66

Following his return to D.C from Sedona, Steven Godfrey paces around his office.

He's a little miffed that TJ Banks stood him up for breakfast, but he's angrier thinking Charlie may have had something to do with her being chased and shot at. He finally picks up the phone and dials.

A woman's voice answers. "Mr. Wilcox's office."

"This is Steven Godfrey with NCI. Let me talk to him."

"One moment please."

Godfrey wipes the sweat off his forehead. He can tell his blood pressure is up by the thumping in his chest, but damn it, this has gone too far. He can't—

A harsh voice comes on the line. "Wilcox."

Godfrey is more than a little intimidated by this man, but he's got to step up. "Charlie, were you responsible for getting TJ Banks shot at?"

"You idiot, not on this line. I'll call you back." Wilcox hangs up with a clunk.

Godfrey blinks in surprise and puts the receiver back on the phone. It rings. An unknown number.

"Charlie, is that—?"

"Goddamn it, Godfrey, you should know better than to speak about our operations on my government line. Did you talk to that Banks woman?"

Godfrey's a bit flustered. "Well, yes, I met with her, and she's considering… but wait a minute, did you arrange those goons to shoot at her?"

"I told you we had resources to take care of things that endanger our projects."

"Look, Charlie, I can't do this anymore. You've gone—"

"Don't be a fool. You *will* continue to do this because you're in too deep. You're in on high-level classified information with the stories I'm handing you on a silver platter. Reel in that Banks woman or your wife may be next when she's on her way to the gym. Do it!"

The line disconnects again. Steven Godfrey sinks onto his office chair and his white-knuckled hands grip the arms. Sweat drips down the side of his cheek. He can tell his blood pressure is spiking. He loosens his necktie and shirt collar.

Stop panicking. Think... think...

Chapter 67

The sleek brushed-steel condo door opens, and Roger's face lights up with a wide smile.

I drop my bags where I stand and melt into my friend's arms.

I hug him a little too long and a little too tight and struggle to keep the tears from escaping my eyes and rolling down my face. *What the hell, it's Roger, he's my buddy, he'll understand and his warmth feels so good and he smells so nice…*

"Hey, TJ, you okay?" Roger says softly, but doesn't let go of me.

I squeeze my eyes closed, give him one more embrace and finally step back. "I've been on a wild ride lately."

Roger nods and picks up my suitcases from the hall as I swipe at my eyes and enter his condominium.

It's been a few years since I've been here, and the place is even more spectacular than I remembered. Outside, through the floor-to-ceiling windows, there's a million-dollar view that goes on forever, the modern downtown Atlanta skyline jutting up into the blue sky. Inside, the contemporary furnishings with a few splashes of color in the living room, tasteful art on the walls, are all stunning yet comfortable. A bar with a fancy metal top looks like it's well stocked with a variety of liquor, and all the correct shapes and sizes of beautiful glassware. Off the kitchen, his computer monitors and desk are visible in a large, neat office. *You could have this, too, if you work for NCI full time.*

I turn, and Roger watches me, brows furrowed. "Sorry, I have a hotel room, but check-in's not 'til later, so I came here straight from the airport."

"It's fine, I'm glad you did. I have a guest room. You're always welcome to stay."

"I don't want to impose…"

"C'mon, TJ, this is me." He takes me by one hand and leads me to a buttery soft white leather sofa. "Please, relax. Want some coffee? Or I have Prosecco, Scotch." He grins.

"Coffee, thanks." I lean back and let the sofa envelop me.

"Black, right?"

He remembers. "Yes, please."

He brings back two steaming mugs and sits beside me. "Talk to me, TJ. Something is going on."

I rub my forehead. "A lot is going on, Rog." I glance at my watch. The digital clock reads 9:30 a.m. I sit up abruptly. "Crap, I'm so sorry. You must be beginning your workday." I start to rise. "I should leave."

Roger takes my arm and pulls me back down. "It's fine. Please, don't go."

Chapter 68

Roger and I talk for hours, like we used to.

I tell him all about the drug bust, getting a bullet through the leg, working with Cho, the migrant child sting, and finally getting chased and shot at in Sedona. I skirt around my relationship with Aaron, only referring to him in a professional manner. Roger gets up once when an urgent email dings on the computer in his office, but he handles it quickly and sits back down again.

He refills our coffee cups a few times, and we eventually turn to the subject of Steven Godfrey.

"I met with him, like I told you I would. And did he ever promise me the moon if I'd come to work full time for NCI. My pick of assignments, my own staff, all the technology available, six-figure salary. He even threw in a luxury apartment in D.C., New York, L.A., wherever I want to be. Even Atlanta." I smile and raise an eyebrow.

Roger nods. "That sounds pretty incredible. Do I hear a 'but' in there?"

I sigh. "There's something about him that's unsettling, just under the surface, like he's hiding something. Maybe it's that source of his who is feeding these stories to him. I need to find out who that is. It might explain why he's so adamant about hiring me at NCI."

"It could also be because you're good at what you do, TJ. Ever think of that?"

I look down at my hands. I've never been one to seek awards or recognition or be in the spotlight. I'm just as happy to be in the background, telling a story with my camera. "Thanks. But there are plenty of other younger reporters who are probably as good, and cheaper."

"Don't downplay your talent and experience." Roger puts down his coffee mug and takes my hand again. "Maybe this would be a good move. I'd really like it if you were here in Atlanta. I miss… being with you."

My eyes prickle with moisture. *I forgot what a nice man Roger is. How we always got along so well. How he always treats me with respect and is fun to be with. But what about Aaron? No. That's over, that's what. What do they say about a "bird in the hand?"*

"We did have some good times, didn't we? Then work and careers kinda got in the way. I've always been so driven…"

"Driven and fearless, TJ. You dive headfirst into everything, ignoring pain, always doing what's right rather than what's easy. But do you really need to work that hard?"

I ponder that. *He knows me very, very well.* "For the first time in my life, maybe not. I've been thinking more and more about settling down in one place, having my own bed, not being on the road all the time." I chuckle. "Is that an age thing?"

Roger smiles. "Maybe. But it might be a 'been there, done that' thing. Time to try something different. See where else life can take you."

We're silent for a moment. "Trouble is, this is all I know. I haven't taken five minutes, let alone five hours, to think about what might be possible."

"How about if we brainstorm tonight? I do need to get back on the desk for a while, but—"

"Oh, of course, I'm so sorry. You must be so busy, and here I'm throwing off your day. I'll go the hotel and get out of your—"

"No. *Please* stay here. The guest room is all ready for you. Unless… you need more privacy…"

"Don't be silly. I just don't want to interrupt—"

"You're not. And you need to chill for a while after everything that's happened." He gets up and takes my bags to the spare room. "Help yourself to anything in the fridge. There's a pool and jacuzzi on the rooftop or the balcony is my favorite place to contemplate."

"You're a good friend." My heart is full. I treasure his friendship.

"I'll take that… for now." He grins.

He wants more. Do I have more to give? More to give to Roger?

"Go back to work. I'll be fine, thanks."

He takes his coffee cup with him and disappears into his office.

Chapter 69

Charles Wilcox pores over documents in his spotless office in the Department of Health and Human Services building on Independence Avenue in Washington, DC.

The soft vibration of a cell phone gets his attention.

A flush comes over his olive skin. He always calls out on that phone. And there's only one person who ever calls in. His hand flies to his face and he gnaws nervously on what's left of his left thumbnail.

A small, thin man, he jumps up, swiftly locks his door and returns to the high-backed chair in front of his upgraded wood desk. He unlocks and opens the skinny middle drawer, where three cell phones sit next to each other. One is a Galaxy Android for government use. The second is an iPhone 13 ProMax for his personal use. The third, a small Nokia burner phone, vibrates. He glances at a little framed mirror on his desk and nervously smooths his graying brown wavy hair, cleverly combed to cover the balding top of his head.

He gulps and presses Answer. "Yes?"

"Charles, vee haf a problem."

The familiar Romanian voice of the person Wilcox knows only as Darkmover speaks calmly, softly.

"If it's about that TV reporter, I'm taking care of it."

There's silence. Too long. Wilcox's breathing speeds up.

"Not vell enough, Charles. She has eenfiltrated von of our operations and I cannot haf dat."

"Not to worry. She's just a gnat." He adjusts his tortoise shell glasses as they slip down his sweaty nose.

More silence. "Von leetle gnat can easily be squashed," Darkmover continues. "But a svarm of gnats can be aggravating and irritating, Charles. Deez gnats now include zee FBI. Vhat you doing about dat?"

"That's easy. It's another government office. I can call them off."

"Easy? Dat's vhat you said about dis TJ Banks voman. Maybe vee should arrange to bring her to me. I vill dispose of her."

Wilcox thinks quickly. *That's not a bad idea. Get her out of my hair.* Then he imagines what Darkmover would probably do to Banks. He gulps. He pulls a handkerchief from his suit pocket and wipes the growing perspiration from his upper lip.

"That's not necessary. I will have another opportunity and it will be done this time."

"See dat eet eez, Charles. I vould not vant to haf you meesing any of your vingers. Or hands."

Wilcox sucks in a gasp. "I assure you. I—"

The click in his ear signals the call has ended.

Wilcox lets out the breath he's been holding. He looks back down at the phone and snaps it shut. He opens it again, presses a button and raises the cell to his ear, chewing on his left thumbnail again.

"Godfrey. Wilcox. That extortion case is going down next week. You *will* get Banks on it, or you will suffer severe consequences. I'll send you the details on our private email." He listens for only a moment. "No excuses. I don't care what you have to do. Just see that it gets done."

Wilcox snaps the phone shut, puts it back in the drawer and locks it. He leans back in his chair and closes his eyes, breathing heavily.

Chapter 70

Roger is spot-on about the peaceful balcony.

I nestle into the soft cushions on the chaise lounge, and it's a lovely place to sit and think with the green cascading plants and colorful flowers everywhere. A soft breeze ruffles the petals of a huge pink azalea in a shiny blue pot. It's a little more humid than Phoenix, but the temperature is perfect, maybe in the mid-70s in the shade. A little bubbly Prosecco helps me relax and I realize I haven't taken many days off, let alone any kind of vacation, in a couple of years.

Financially, I can certainly afford to take time off work. I guess it's the freelancer's conundrum of never really knowing when or if your next assignment will come and never wanting to say no to a gig.

Just when I start to imagine my life here in Atlanta, in a home of my own, perhaps focusing only on sex-trafficking assignments, Steven Godfrey's words swirl in my head. I ponder him and his "source."

I need to find out who is feeding him the information. Must be someone close to the government to get me into the inside circle of the DEA, FBI and other big agencies. Depending on who he or she is, maybe they could help me infiltrate bigger sex-trafficking operations. That could be my life's work. Not the bloody crime scenes that repeat over and over again. To focus on this important story… expose these bastard traffickers to the world… to rescue more women and boys and girls… find Katrina so we can be best friends again…

"Hey, sleeping beauty." Roger's voice is soft, and it comes from the chair next to mine.

I open my eyes and realize I must've dozed off. The temperature has dropped a few degrees with the late afternoon sun, and Roger probably put the soft white blanket over me. I stretch. "Mmmm… how long have I been out?"

"A few hours. But I realized neither one of us has eaten much today, and I don't know about you, but I'm starving."

Coffee, bubbly and a handful of grapes from Roger's refrigerator is all I've had since dinner last night. Was I in Sedona just yesterday? It seems like an eternity ago.

"You're right. I'm famished, too. What do you suggest?"

"A favorite eatery down the block. We've got reservations in a half hour. Is that enough time for you?"

"Sure. Let me jump in the shower and change and I'll be ready."

Roger starts to stand, but I take his arm. He sits back down and turns to look at me.

"Did I tell you thanks?"

"For what?"

"Are you kidding? For listening to me rant, for letting me stay, for giving me a lovely place to nap… the list goes on."

"You're welcome." A pause. "I'm glad you're here, TJ. And it's good to have a conversation with you that lasts more than five minutes." He gives me a peck on the cheek. "More of that to come. Go get dressed."

The hotel room cancelled, I've unpacked the few clothes I brought and for the first time in a long time, place them neatly in the dresser drawers in Roger's spare room rather than pulling them haphazardly from my open suitcase as needed. The short stroll to the restaurant is lovely, with a soft, warm breeze around us.

I didn't realize how hungry I am. We have a wonderful dinner, with appetizers, entrées and dessert, interspersed with rambling conversations that include some shop talk, travels we've both been on, foods we like and don't like, but nothing very serious. *It's almost like we're getting to know each other again.*

Yet I feel… uneasy. Maybe it's just his nearness. Maybe I shouldn't have mentioned the extortion case Godfrey's offering. Maybe it's—

"That's about the fifth time you've looked at your watch," Roger interrupts gently. "You gotta be somewhere?"

"I'm sorry, no…" *What is it?* "For some reason, I'm… restless. It's like I'm forgetting to do something, like I need to research my next assignment, book a hotel room, catch a flight, shoot my next story."

"You're probably not used to being in one place for more than a few minutes," Roger suggests.

"Yes, that's probably it." I shake my head. "Is this how you live? Work 9 to 5, then have evenings and weekends to yourself? Who does that in the news business?"

"Yes, believe it or not, some people don't work 24/7/365 like you," Roger says with a grin. "There are these things called 'days off' and 'vacations' and places like movie theatres and museums and parks where people go in their non-working hours."

I smile. "Yeah, guess that's all kinda foreign to me. I've been on my own, making my own money and creating my own schedule for so long…" I pause. "But it's tiring."

"I know the feeling. And trust me, I put in a lot of long hours most of the time." He looks down. "But maybe that's because…"

"You need to fill up those empty hours and days because there's no one to share them with?"

Roger looks up at me, a wistful, sad expression on his face, and he nods.

"I know that feeling, too." I take his hand across the restaurant table. "And I sense… a shift, a change coming. I'm not sure exactly what it's going to be or where I'll end up, but… this feels so good. For now, anyway."

Roger squeezes my hand. "Then let's not put any pressure on ourselves and just enjoy it… one day at a time."

A beat. "That's a little schmaltzy, don't you think?" I ask.

"Yeah, I knew that the minute it came out!" We both laugh.

And head out into the soft night air, arm in arm.

Chapter 71

Roger eases out of bed, careful not to wake TJ, sleeping soundly on his king bed.

Her short hair is flat on one side, her hands clutch the sheet and blanket under her chin, and her gold necklace streams down the back of her neck.

He smiles as he quietly pads to the kitchen to brew coffee, remembering the night before. Amazing dinner, deep discussions he hasn't had with anyone else for a long time, feeling so comfortable with her.

Don't get your hopes up. I don't think she's the settling-down kind. Despite her talk, Roger wonders if TJ is "trying it on for size" to see how staying in one place feels. But will she really make a move to a full-time position, a house or condo, and no more living out of a suitcase?

They talked until almost midnight while relaxing on the patio, enjoying the cool evening air and the lights twinkling from the city below and the stars above. He kissed her goodnight—not a peck, and nothing too forceful, just soft and gentle—and they went to their own rooms.

But it wasn't long before he heard his bedroom door open, and next thing he knew she is sliding in next to him, her warm naked body curling up against his. It didn't feel like four years since they'd been in bed together. Rather it felt natural and good and right. They made love and this morning Roger started imagining her with him all the time, working together again, cooking dinners together again, maybe getting married—

Stop. Don't get carried away. Don't let your near-celibacy for the past few years adversely color what this is: two friends who haven't seen each other for a while.

He fills a mug with coffee and sits at his computer to start his day.

Chapter 72

"**I**'m gonna take the extortion job," I announce at Roger's office door, wearing one of his oversized Atlanta Braves T-shirts.

"Well, good morning to you, too." Roger removes the telephone earpiece from around his head and leans back in his leather chair, hands folded across his chest. No smile.

Oops. Probably not the most appropriate greeting, considering the night before. Roger's jaw is set and his face has lost the loving looks he gave me while we were having sex.

"Sorry. Good morning." I walk to his chair, cup my hands around his square jaw and give him a light kiss, his overnight stubble tickling my lips. I run my hand over his short hair. *He's gotten grayer since I saw him last. Which makes him even better looking.* "Thanks for letting me sleep. How long have you been up?"

Roger glances at his watch. "A couple of hours. Catching up from yesterday."

"I'm sorry if I put you behind. I—"

"Stop apologizing. It's all right. Now what made you decide to do the extortion story?"

I pause. "Got coffee?"

He finally grins. "Of course." He stands up and grabs his cup and I follow him to his kitchen. The black cabinets contrast with the light gray and white granite countertops and stainless-steel appliances. Contemporary square light fixtures hang from the ceiling and there are splashes of red: a toaster, a ceramic holder for utensils, even a red coffeemaker.

"Beautiful," I say, looking around. "Never really gave much thought to kitchens being so much more than just functional."

He gets another mug from a cabinet, pours my coffee and refills his. He leans against the counter. "Wanna fill me in on your decision?"

I take a sip, inhaling the luscious aroma of roasted coffee beans. "It's not so much the specific story as it is a way to find out who Godfrey's 'source' is."

"Is that so important?"

"I'm not sure, but I think it might be. It's just a gut feeling. It's too… suspicious."

"Okay," Roger says tentatively. "The extortion case is happening in Vegas. How are you going to find out about his contact?"

"I'll tell Godfrey the only way I'll take the story is if I can meet this guy. He'll probably say no, which means the assignment won't happen. If he says yes, I'll be able to get a feel for where his source is coming from."

Roger looks uneasy as he gazes down at his cup. "I don't know, TJ. He's probably just some low-level bureaucrat who stumbles on a juicy lead now and then."

"But he could also be a higher-level bureaucrat who knows a lot more. I want to find out."

"I'm pretty sure you're not asking my permission." He looks squarely into my eyes.

I open my mouth, close it again. "I do value your judgment, Roger."

"You're talking about two separate decisions. One is meeting this guy, which if it makes you feel more comfortable, go for it. The other is taking the extortion story, which could be dangerous."

"Right. But half my gigs have an element of danger. Comes with the territory."

"Please note that while I'd like to try to talk you out of it, I won't."

"Thanks. I appreciate it." *He knows how stubborn I can be.* "And there's something you said earlier. Doing what's right rather than what's easy. I think you nailed it."

"It's a noble mission, TJ. But not at your own expense."

"But then whose?"

Chapter 73

Roger is silent. It's a rhetorical question, and we're both fully cognizant of it.

The mission is the priority.

I check my watch. "I'm going to call Godfrey, then make flight arrangements to D.C."

Roger's eyebrows go up, and he looks hopeful. "You're welcome to use this as your base."

"That would be great, thank you."

"And will you please just keep me updated?" He pauses. "Sorry, that sounded a little, uh, possessive." He chuckles. "Just send me a text occasionally. You know I care about you."

I put my coffee down and walk to him. "I will. And the feeling is mutual, Roger." I give him a tender kiss, the "we're-more-than-friends-but-I-don't-know-how-much-more" kind. I turn away, trying not to notice his expression.

I'm in the waiting area outside Steve Godfrey's office at News Crews International in Washington, D.C.

It's tasteful, but a bit opulent. Lots of beige with touches of gold trim, gold curtains draped open at the windows, gold piping on the chairs.

Godfrey's door opens. "T.J., what a nice surprise!" his voice booms. "Please, come in."

I follow him into his office, where he closes the door and gives me his too big bear hug. "It's so good to see you!"

I manage to extricate myself and walk around the office. The gold touches from outside continue here, which is probably an indication of Godfrey's elevated opinion of himself.

"I hope you're going to tell me you're ready to come work for NCI full time," he says, indicating a gold brocade chair for me to sit on. He takes the one next to me, rather than the office chair behind his desk.

"I do want to talk to you about the position," I start. "I would also—"

"That's great news!" He almost looks giddy. He pats my leg a few times then leaves his hand there. "We can get all the paperwork started and—"

I stand up and walk to the window. "First I would like to meet your source for the last drug bust and the upcoming extortion story." I turn to watch his reaction.

He blinks a couple of times, and the color drains from his ruddy face. He swallows. "Uh, I don't think… I mean, I don't see any reason why that would be necessary. He—"

"It's just a comfort-level thing for me." I try to keep my tone light. "I want to understand where he's getting his information, how reliable it is."

"Hey, he works for the government, how much more reliable can it be?" Godfrey forces a chuckle. "I don't think we need to bother him. We'll get all the details we need. Now, let's get you down to Human Resources first—"

"I'm not taking the extortion case unless I meet him."

Chapter 74

Steven Godfrey stands up, walks to his desk and paces behind it, head down. *What the fuck? There's no way. Charlie'd probably do god-knows-what to her right there in his office. Then it would be on my conscience. Wait. Maybe I'd be off the hook then. Let Charlie deal with her. Maybe he wouldn't do anything untoward in a government building. Would he?*

He turns back to TJ and forces a smile. "Well, let me see if I can reach him. He's a busy guy." Godfrey reaches for his desktop handset, hesitates, and opens his top desk drawer. He hesitates again, closes the drawer and picks up the office phone receiver instead. He punches a button. "Call Charlie Wilcox for me." He sits in his leather chair. "While we're waiting, let's talk about where—"

His phone rings. He picks it up, listens. "Charlie, how are you?"

"Goddamn it, Godfrey, I told you not to—"

"Putting you on speaker, Charlie." He punches a button. "Guess who I have in my office. TJ Banks, and she'd like to meet you."

There's a beat of silence. *Oh, shit, what have I done?*

"Ms. Banks." Charlie's voice comes across calmly, with that annoying nasal sound. "This *is* a surprise. I'm a big fan of your work."

TJ walks toward the desk. "I appreciate you getting me on the L.A. drug sting. But before I take on the extortion assignment, I'd like to meet you. In person. I'm here in D.C. What would be a good time?"

Another few seconds of silence. Godfrey gulps. He wipes the sweat off his forehead. *I hope I'm doing the right thing …*

"Well, as luck would have it," Charlie continues, "I have a few minutes later this afternoon for a quick appointment. Why don't you come around, say, 5:30?"

Oh, damn, that's after government hours. His staff will probably be gone. Am I sending her to a terrible fate? How do I—

"That will be perfect, Mr. Wilcox. Now, you're in the Department of Health and Human Services on Independence, right?"

"More *orrr* less." He chuckles. "Inside joke. ORR. Office of Refugee Resettlement."

Chapter 75

Ding, *ding, ding* go the bells in my head, like a bunch of old-time alarm clocks going off at once.

Charlie Wilcox. Office of Refugee Resettlement. "More *orrr* less." *What the hell does that mean?*

"Thank you, Mr. Wilcox. I'll see you then."

"Talk to you later, Charlie." A visibly nervous Godfrey disconnects the line with a shaking hand. He leans back in his chair, breathing heavily.

"Steve, are you all right?"

"Oh, sure, just, uh, excited about you coming on board."

"Let me meet with Mr. Wilcox first, then we'll talk more." I head swiftly toward the door, anxious to get out of there. "I'll be in touch."

Godfrey stays plopped in his chair, looking wiped. He doesn't get up.

As I race down the hall, I shake off the creepy feeling that always lingers after I see or speak to Steven Godfrey.

I've got some time before my meeting with Wilcox. That will give me an opportunity to find out more about the man, now that I have a name.

I find a coffee shop with free Wi-Fi, set up my laptop with VPN and start searching.

This can't be a coincidence.

It's two hours later and I've determined that Charles Wilcox is a besieged mid-level bureaucrat who seems to consider himself a player.

He attends big functions like the annual Dream Big Charity dinner, the White House Correspondents Dinner and other galas in D.C. and at the White House. He's divorced, no children, has an undergrad from Wharton's and started an online Master of Science program in Finance at Georgetown, but never finished it.

But more unsettling is where he works. He heads up the Office of Refugee Resettlement, which goes by the acronym ORR, which places migrant children in shelters until they are released to a family member, guardian or foster family. ORR has been pressured by families, media, the administration to get those children reunited with their parents, with only limited success.

Can Wilcox be the same government official running a sex-trafficking ring with some of those children? He would certainly be in the right position to do so. But he couldn't do it by himself. If he is the one, who else is he working with? And could that be why he is dangling these carrot stories for me—drug sting, extortion ring—to steer me *away* from sex-trafficking investigations?

Of course, I have no proof. Yet.

I need Cho.

Cho is in her huge spaceship chair, wearing her headphones as we video chat.

She sits in her usual place, today wearing a coral and gray kimono, large beverage by her side. The California sun streams in through her kitchen window.

"Yes, it possible to hack most any phone. Depends what information you looking for."

"I mostly need phone numbers, Cho. I want to find out who is helping this guy."

"You have physical access to the phone?"

I hesitate. "Doubt it. I can't imagine he'd use his office or regular cell phone for illegal dealings, so I'm guessing there's a burner phone somewhere. But I'm pretty sure he won't let me borrow it."

"Sniffing a Wi-Fi network could work. I send—"

"Wait, 'sniffing Wi-Fi'? What does that mean?"

"It means capturing information traveling over a Wi-Fi network. If you close to the phone, I set you up with software to punch hole in his wireless system."

"You are amazing, Cho!"

"No. Like I tell you before, I have my tricks."

Cho sets up the necessary sniffing software on my phone.

I realize I don't have to tell her to be careful, but warn her this may be an extremely dangerous person.

I also clip on a thumb-size mini wireless camera to a cotton shirt I wear over my black T-shirt. The tiny lens of the camera is positioned through a buttonhole to record my conversation with Wilcox.

I've got one more call to make. And it's not going to be an easy one.

Some people think I'm brave to take part in a drug sting operation or to cover a deadly crime or a traumatic incident.

It's mostly for the thrill of great video, but I'll admit sometimes I'm naïve or even stupid to take on certain stories.

Right now, I feel no bravery at all. Instead, there's a combination of embarrassment, anger and a myriad of other senseless emotions when it comes to talking to FBI Agent Aaron Porter.

I hail a taxi on the street to Wilcox's office. The entire way in the cab I start to dial him but stop every time.

Outside the Federal building on Independence Avenue, I finally chicken out and text him instead:

U might want to ck out Charles Wilcox in the Office of Refugee Resettlement, which goes by O-R-R. The office places migrant children in shelters until they are released to a family member, guardian or foster family. He might be part of the sex trafficking ring we busted in Phx. More orrr less.

Text sent, I silence my phone and pocket it before heading in to meet Charles Wilcox.

Chapter 76

Aaron Porter is half asleep in a dull meeting with the Child Exploitation and Human Trafficking Task Force group in the New York Bureau office.

They've not made much progress, and the leader of the group is rehashing the same tired information.

Porter's mind wanders to TJ Banks. He's still pissed off as hell at her but regrets the shouting match they got into in Phoenix. *I fully understand she was trying to help. But at her own personal risk. Doesn't she get that? When will she ever learn that—*

His cell vibrates in his pocket. The head of the task force, an older woman with short, graying brown hair and a voice that tends to drone, is reading statistics about child sex trafficking. He pulls out his phone and internally shakes his head seeing a text from TJ Banks.

He looks up. Everyone stares at a digital slideshow on the screen. He taps the text message and reads it. He stops at the "more orrr less."

What the hell? Porter's adrenaline spikes. *Where have I heard that phrase?* He searches his memory banks and then: the kid from the migrant trafficking house in Phoenix.

He gathers his things and stands. "Excuse me, but I've got an urgent matter that just came up." He swiftly leaves the room and heads to his cubicle. He punches TJ's number as he walks. It continues to ring until her voicemail picks up.

"This is TJ, leave me a message."

"Banks, it's Porter. Got your text. Call me right away. I think there's a connection."

He reaches his office, opens his laptop and searches for the transcript of the interview with the young man, a Jared Jordon, who was in charge of the children overnight at the Phoenix house. *There it is:*

Porter: Is there anything else you can tell us?

Jordon: Well, some of the guys would joke about the dude they got instructions from, saying he was "more orrr less" a puppet for someone else. Then they'd all laugh. I didn't know what they were talking about.

Porter calls TJ again. "Banks, where are you? Call me back. Now!"

He hopes she is either still in Phoenix or maybe has gone to L.A. with her cyber friend. He races back to the conference room to update his team.

Chapter 77

It's go time.

I reach Wilcox's office about a half hour ahead of schedule and surveil the plain lobby area outside his office, which is marked "Director." I watch as a 50-something woman gathers her oversized purse, lunch bag and sweater from the back of her chair to leave her post right on the dot of 5 p.m. The rest of the area is empty.

As she walks by me, I pretend to be waiting outside a hallway door, just another person nonchalantly checking her cell phone. I see a couple of text messages and voicemails from Aaron, but don't have time to look at them now. *Gotta stay focused.*

I pull up the sniffing software Cho provided me with and activate it. It displays a variety of Wi-Fi networks, including the government internet, three Bluetooth printers and several cell phones. I click to Select All.

Another app on my phone shows the view from my button-hole camera, and I press Record to start the video.

I walk to his office, take a big breath and knock on the door.

After a few seconds, Wilcox's door swings open and there's the briefest flash of irritation in the dark squinting eyes of the short, wiry man on the other side. His face adjusts to a bland, expressionless look.

"You must be Ms. Banks," he says, a nasal quality to his voice.

"Sorry, I'm early. I can wait out here…"

"Um, no, it's quite all right. Come in."

Wilcox rushes back to his desk, and I follow him inside the basic bland taupe painted government office where everything is immaculate and in its place. Books shelved neatly. Papers stacked perfectly. Even his in and out boxes are tidy. The top of his dark wood desk shines in the overhead fluorescent lights, with only three items occupying the space: a long, green stone nameplate with CHARLES WILCOX engraved in oversized letters; a black leather desk pad, devoid of any papers; and a small stone desk frame facing his chair not with a photo, but with… a mirror.

"Please, sit." He nods toward three padded chairs opposite him, and I take the one closest to the door. He dips his head slightly for a quick look in his mirror. His hand quickly swipes over his hair.

Who looks at themselves like that? He doesn't seem like the type to be so concerned with his appearance. "I appreciate your seeing me on short notice." I take out a pad of paper and a pen. "I'm very interested in the extortion case," I lie, "and would like to find out more about what your office does." That part is true. *And whether you are responsible for a migrant child sex-trafficking ring.*

"As for the case in Las Vegas, Godfrey can provide all the details."

"I'm mostly interested in *where* you are getting your information."

"Why is that important?"

"Well, with my assignments from NCI, I'm confident all the elements have been vetted and doublechecked and are solid. I don't know you well yet, so I just need to make sure the same attention to detail is being followed."

"I can assure you I work only with the highest levels in the United States government." He pulls a side desk drawer and removes a green file folder, opening it carefully, straightening the papers inside. "Now, this involves several white-collar criminals in—"

I don't give a shit about that case. "Actually, you're right," I interrupt. "I can get the rest of the info from Steve at NCI. Why don't we talk about your work here? Would you tell me more about what your office does?"

He closes the file. "Is this an interview?" His thumb goes to his teeth and he chews on his nail for a second, then quickly lowers his hand.

"Is that a problem?"

He pauses a moment, as if searching carefully for his words. "I want to be certain this is not one of those 'gotcha' interviews that some so-called journalists pull."

"That's not my style." *At the moment.* "This can be on background." I put down my paper and pen and wait for him to answer.

"We're just another government agency. I thought we were talking about—"

"But it's a very important office, given the recent border issues." My reporter hat on, I try to ease in slowly. "Can you tell me how many migrant children you've been able to reunite with their parents in the past two years?"

"I'll have to find the latest information and get back with you. Now, about the extortion situation—"

He's going to stonewall me. Time to dive in. "Mr. Wilcox, are you also aware that there have been at least two instances where migrant children were placed into sex-trafficking houses rather than the foster homes where they were supposed to go?"

His jaw clenches, the only visible change in his face I can detect. "*If* that happened, and I think it's *extremely* unlikely, it *certainly* would not be from my office." He promptly stands up. "I was not prepared to discuss anything but the extortion case, so speak with my secretary and she can make an appointment for you." Wilcox ushers me out the door.

There's no way I'll ever hear from her. "But did you know—"

"I have no more time to talk now. Good day, Ms. Banks." He quickly shuts the door.

I leave the lobby and turn the corner into the empty hallway and stop. I hope Wilcox will pick up the burner phone to call his contact, so I need to stay close by. I open the software on my phone.

Sure enough, a telephone number without any caller ID is "sniffed," along with the digits on a long number he's calling.

With a +40 European country dialing code. *Where is that?*

Chapter 78

Charles Wilcox purses his lips into a thin line as he listens for his call to go through.

"Yes, Charles?" comes Darkmover's voice on his burner phone.

"You're right again, as always," Wilcox brownnoses. "I will arrange to send TJ Banks to you in Romania. That will get her out of my way, and I'm sure you have many more resources at your disposal than I."

"Vhy zee sudden change, Charles? I thought you ver handling it."

"She's too close. And here in the U.S., any, uh, change in her status would *not* go unnoticed. Europe, however, is a different story…"

"Very well, Charles." Darkmover pauses. "Zees vill be qvite exciting. Here's vhat vee must do…"

Wilcox lets out a breath. *And I can get Darkmover off my ass as well. I don't need this toxic relationship anymore. I've got my operation right where I want it…* He barely listens to the instructions.

Chapter 79

Romania.

I'm back at the coffee shop with my laptop and find +40 is the Romanian country code for the call Charles Wilcox made after he abruptly ended our meeting. *Why would a U.S. government official call someone in Romania? And who would that be?* The country is certainly one of the top 10 places where sex trafficking runs rampant. That's got to be the connection, but I need evidence.

And I can't do this on my own. *Gotta call Porter.*

Three voicemails. Just the thought of him speeds up my heartbeat, and despite the shouting match we got into last time I saw him in Phoenix, there's that warm tingle in my stomach. I tap on his number.

Sugar, not vinegar, Banks. You can do this.

He picks up on the first ring. "Where have you been, Banks? I've been trying to reach you. It's—"

"I know, I know. Look, I'm really sorry about how things ended between us. But I—"

"That doesn't matter right now. It's about Charles Wilcox. Like you said, it's very possible he's connected to the migrant house in Phoenix."

Wasn't expecting that. Instead of scolding me again, he's agreeing with me? "I can't prove it yet, though. You found something?"

"Maybe. It was a phrase you wrote in your text. The 'more orrr less' line."

I'm stumped. "I think that's just a juvenile inside joke his office uses for—"

"They're not the only ones who use it. Remember the kid we arrested at the Phoenix sex-trafficking house? He said something I didn't quite understand at the time, but now I do. He said he and his fellow traffickers would joke about the man they got instructions from, saying he was 'more *orrr* less' a puppet for someone else, then they'd laugh. They'd emphasize and elongate the *orrr* just like you did."

A bolt of adrenaline hits my system. "Shit, then this *must* be the guy running that operation. I had hoped to have more proof when I met with him—"

"Wait, what are you talking about?"

"I just saw Wilcox in his D.C. office. Turns out he's the one who's been feeding those big stories to me through NCI. First it was the L.A. drug sting, and now he has some extortion-ring case for me. I told NCI I wouldn't take it unless I met Wilcox in person. I think he's been trying to distract me from the sex-trafficking stories, so I thought I could get him to talk."

A snide chuckle from Aaron. "And you thought he would blurt out, 'Yes, I'm the mastermind behind the migrant kids being sold?' What were you think— Wait, that's just it, once again you're not thinking. Look, we—"

"Hold on." *Damnit, here we go again.* "If I had told you I thought he was involved, you would've dismissed it."

"If you would've called me back earlier, I would've confirmed it."

There's silence. *Are we at an impasse?*

I shake my head to clear it. "So, what do we do?"

"There's no 'we' in this scenario, TJ." Aaron's voice is softer. "You need to let the FBI and my team take care of him. I'll keep you in the loop, and you can be the first one with the story."

This time I'm the one who is silent for a moment. "I think he's the tip of the iceberg."

"Meaning?"

"Meaning, I have good reason to believe he's working with someone in Romania, and I'd guess it's also about selling kids for sex."

"The Bureau doesn't deal in guesswork. Where is your intel coming from?"

"Don't ask me how I got it, but I have a number in that country that Wilcox called right after our meeting. My *gut* tells me they're connected. Are you telling me you don't work off your instincts?"

"At times, yes, but we need facts, proof. I assure you—"

"That the Bureau will take its sweet time in getting the facts and proof and meanwhile kids are treated like sex slaves? I'm going to—"

"Stand down, Banks." *There's that stern voice.* "This is not your job. Let it go."

"Is that a command, Porter? I'm not one of your minions, and I don't like to be ordered around. I—"

"You're a civilian, and it's for your own damned safety! Why can't you see that?"

There's that safety word again. He'll never understand me.

"This is what I see, Aaron." My voice is almost a whisper. "I will do what's right. Not what's easy." I disconnect the line.

With an even greater resolve than ever.

Chapter 80

I reserve a room in an Arlington hotel. I could go back to Atlanta, but somehow, I feel the need to stay close to Wilcox.

And I just can't face Roger after the conversation with Porter. I'm frustrated with Aaron, but there are still strong personal feelings involved. Feelings I can't deal with right now.

I text Cho on the PGP line to have her check out the Romanian phone number.

I should call Roger, but text him instead:

Good mtg with Wilcox. Might have found a connection. Staying in DC tonite.

How can I catch Charles Wilcox in the act of moving migrant kids into what I believe are his own sex trafficking houses? He's got to be working with others. Maybe I can follow him, take photos, see who he meets with. Does he know I'm on to him? If so, he'll probably be extra cautious. If not, maybe I can—

My cell rings. It's Steven Godfrey. *Shit. He's going to want an answer about coming to work full-time for NCI, plus about the extortion story. How long can I keep putting him off?*

I consider letting it go to voicemail, then click answer. "Banks."

"TJ!" Godfrey's voice booms in my ear. "Glad I caught you. Got a minute? Want to talk with you about a couple of—"

"Steve, I haven't made a decision about NCI or the extortion story yet, so—"

"Oh, that's okay. Extortion assignment is on hold. New subject. Charlie Wilcox said you two had a good meeting, and—"

"He did?" I interrupt. *Do I tell him I practically got thrown out of his office? Or let on to Godfrey that Wilcox may be the corrupt government official I've been looking for?* "What did he say exactly?"

"Called me a few minutes ago. That he understands your interest in sex trafficking—personally I do *not* want to think about those bastards—and he has a new lead for you."

"What kind of a lead?" I say cautiously, my stomach twisting.

"This could be a super big story, TJ. He says he can put us directly on the trail of a major organization for sex trafficking of women and children in Europe. Sounds like if you are successful in breaking up this ring, it would be a major coup not just for NCI but for Europe as well the United States because there may be connections here. Whaddaya say? It would mean a trip for you across the pond."

My head reels. *The chance to go after a vast operation. One with potentially international ties. Think of all the young girls and boys we could save. But is Wilcox the connection—?*

"You still there, TJ?"

"Uh, yeah, and I'm definitely interested. I'm still in D.C. I'll come by the office and get the details."

"Atta girl. See you soon."

This could be it.

The holy grail of sex trafficking. A chance to free so many abused women and innocent children from the bonds of sex slavery. Expose the evil behind it. Make an international example out of them.

But is Wilcox connected to this group as well? Why would he rat on his source?

And when do I bring Porter in on this one? It's no secret the FBI often works with Europol on international crimes. But he'll just say, "We'll handle it" and I'm left on the sidelines.

No, I'll get in close, then I'll call him.

This time while I'm in Godfrey's office, I hardly notice the gold everything.

I'm uber focused on this latest, very important assignment.

Godfrey says I'm going to Bucharest, the capital city of Romania. Once there, Wilcox has contact information for someone who knows the location for the international sex trafficker's base of operations.

"The person who runs this organization moves around a lot, so Wilcox says his people will do surveillance to find them."

"Don't we want to go to one of the actual trafficking houses? Where women and children are being kept? What pictures am I going to get in an office?"

"There will probably be records and other details about the operation there. Probably a lot of other people who are complicit as well."

My cell vibrates in my pocket, but I ignore it. *This is not sitting well. There are too many variables.* "Are you sure we can trust Wilcox? And this contact of his?"

"I asked the same thing. He assured me his information is solid. I would not send you into something that I wasn't convinced was legit. That's why I've also talked to Roger Lester, and he's going with you to produce."

"What? Why? No!" A jumble of emotions course through me in a matter of a few seconds. *Alarm. Gratefulness. Concern for Roger. Fear.*

"I realize you're normally a one woman band, but this is too big to send you by yourself. And once you and Roger are on the ground there and have the traffickers in your sights, Wilcox will send in the FBI and local law enforcement."

Of course, that's the way it should be done. Did I think I could just waltz in and single-handedly take down a heinous, multi-country trafficking operation? But I can't put Roger at risk. "No way are we involving Roger. It could be dangerous."

"Not up for discussion. Did you forget Roger was a reporter embedded in Afghanistan with a Marine Corps troop on the front lines? He's seen danger. More reason to send him."

Oh. He's right. I'll have his back and he'll have mine.

"Okay." I feel my shoulders loosen as a sense of relief washes over me. "It will be good to work with him again."

"And get a load of this guy's name in Romania." Godfrey rustles through some papers as my phone buzzes again. I look at it, and it's a message from Cho.

Number belongs to Darkmover.

Godfrey says, "He goes by the name 'Darkmover.'"

Chapter 81

My head spins on the flight back to Atlanta.
I don't tell Godfrey that Cho and her hackers have had their eyes on Darkmover all along. That Aaron and the FBI have been looking into that name as well. That it pretty much cements the working relationship between Darkmover and Charles Wilcox.

Exactly what is their arrangement? That Darkmover's trafficking operation expanded from Europe into the United States, thanks to Charles Wilcox? That Wilcox would supply migrant children to Darkmover's disgusting enterprise? Were some of the migrant children brought across the U.S. border, then sent to another *country,* all in the name of the lucrative sex-slave trade? And who are the slimy coyotes here and abroad helping Wilcox traffic these kids?

But if he's been working with Darkmover, is Wilcox now throwing the trafficker under the bus? Maybe Wilcox has a shred of ethics and is going to do the right thing? Or maybe he's feeling emboldened and doesn't need Darkmover's help anymore?

It's a lot to process, and I have a dull headache from it.

Or it could be the straight Scotch I slugged on the plane.

"We're going to Romania?"

Roger's face exudes excitement along with a sense of bewilderment as he lets me into his condo.

"Yeah, crazy, right?" I drop my bag inside the door and head to the sofa. "Got something to drink?"

Roger glances at a shiny chrome clock on the wall. "Uh, it's only 10:30 in the morning."

"It's 5 o'clock somewhere."

Roger's eyebrows rise. He fixes me a drink at the bar.

"Hey, you gonna make me drink alone?"

"I need to keep my wits about me on this one." He sits across from me. "Let's talk."

I take a sip of Scotch, then blow out a big breath.

"This is big, Roger. And while normally I would jump in feet first, this time…" I shake my head. "I have a… an uneasy feeling about it."

"Then say no to—"

"Don't get me wrong, I want to go. Desperately. It could be the most important work I do." I look straight into Roger's eyes. "But I want your help. I *need* your help."

"If you think we can pull it off, I'm good to go." He returns a stern gaze. "But you've got to let me in on *everything*. Nothing left out. Can you do that?"

Everything? Sure, Darkmover. Wilcox. But what about Aaron?

"Of course. That's the only way."

"All right. Let's do it."

Three hours later, and I've laid out everything for Roger.

All the conversations with Godfrey and Wilcox. What I suspect about Darkmover. About FBI Special Agent Aaron Porter's involvement with the Bureau's Child Exploitation and Human Trafficking Task Force, the migrant house sting in Phoenix and his search for Darkmover.

"There's something else I need to tell you about Aaron."

The use of his first name doesn't go unnoticed by Roger. "Go on."

I look down at my hands. "We've had… a relationship of sorts for a few years. It runs hot and cold. I think we might have something, then we practically come to blows and it's a mess. We're very different people."

"Do you love him?"

The question takes me by surprise. When I look up, Roger has an almost sad, wistful look on his face.

"I… " *Be honest. Let him in. Tell him everything. Even if it hurts him.* "I'm not sure. Maybe." *And that's the truth.* "But I can't let that get in the way of this operation. As Godfrey said, we will need to bring him in once we get to Bucharest and have something solid." I pause a moment. "Are you sure you're good with all this? You don't have to go. I don't want to do anything that would damage our friendship."

Roger scoffs. "So, we're back to friends with benefits?"

"Please, Rog, let's not do this right now. You and I go way back. We have a great relationship. Always have."

"But you don't feel the same way about me."

"I don't know that either." *Could I love Roger? I think so. We have so much more in common than I do with Aaron. He is probably so much better for me than Aaron. Except...*

"I love you in so many ways. And maybe we just need to let this play out and see where it goes. Never say never, Roger."

He sighs. "Again, I guess I'll take that... for now."

Chapter 82

Roger makes all the arrangements for flights, hotel, transport to the airport, a vehicle and a translator in Bucharest.

I realize how great it is to have a producer again. Allows me to concentrate on the story itself, getting great footage, writing and editing a killer piece. Flashbacks flood back of my time working—and playing—with Roger right here in Atlanta when we both worked for CNN.

Back then we'd cover anything they sent us on: F-scale tornadoes in the Midwest; an airliner crash with only a few survivors; the sexual-harassment case of a major tech CEO. Roger was always a few steps ahead, efficient, anticipating, and rarely did he say, "We can't do that." It was always, "Let me see what I can do," and he always did. We were a team. *Could we be a team again? And in ways other than work?*

Roger dashes over to the Atlanta NCI office to pick up some equipment, while I videochat with Cho about going to Bucharest and her hacker sources who found Darkmover.

"How confident are you these guys have good intel?" I've switched to black coffee and take a sip.

"They very good at what they do." Cho's colored nails work her keyboard as her face stays glued to the monitors. "They tell me this Darkmover has very sophisticated system of electronics that can be packed up and moved within half an hour."

"So, do they have a current location?"

"They watching to confirm, but 90% certain, yes."

"Supposedly Charles Wilcox with the government does as well, but I'm leery of him. But if they both point to the same spot, then we'll be good."

Cho turns to look directly at the camera, and thus at me, and her serious face is more somber than usual. Her bright red kimono belies her tone. "Be very careful of Wilcox. He not good guy."

"I know. You're right."

"We also close to finding person who helps him."

I was so focused on Darkmover, I had forgotten about the others he must be working with. "That's amazing, Cho. Who is it?"

"Not sure yet. Might be former pimp."

I nod. "Figures. Who better than an experienced trafficker?"

The condo door opens and Roger strides in, silver metal pelican equipment cases in each hand.

"Cho, I gotta run, but I'll be in close contact with you all the way."

"Be careful, TJ." Cho admonishes, then clicks off the camera. A feeling of dread twists my stomach.

I shake it off and join Roger in the living room, where he's spread out a bunch of electronic gear.

"What's all this?" I'm a gadget girl, and it's a thrill to see all these shiny toys.

"Just the best and smallest equipment for covert audio recording, a variety of hidden video recording devices, tracking devices, even a working flashlight with a stun gun hidden inside that delivers a 15-million-volt charge."

My eyebrows go up. "Wow."

"We may not need it, but we gotta be prepared for anything, TJ." He hands me a small white velvet box, the kind that holds engagement rings.

What the hell? In the middle of looking at spy gear and he's giving me a gift? I don't reach for it. "What's that?"

Roger gives a little grin. "Don't get so freaked out. Just open it up."

I can tell I'm blushing, as the temperature in my body feels like it shoots up 10 degrees. I reluctantly take the little soft square and flip up the top. It's a beautiful pair of tiny diamond pierced earrings. *Shit, it is a present.* "Roger, I can't accept—"

"They're not real diamonds, just CZs. And there's a tracking device in them."

I suddenly feel even more embarrassed. "Oh. Wow. That's amazing, Roger."

Roger takes out his cell phone and taps a few keys, then shows me a flashing red dot on his screen. "Just in case we get separated or…

something." The smile on his face disappears and he's suddenly serious. "I'm not gonna lie to you. This could get dicey."

"I understand." The danger element has been rumbling deep inside my body since I first heard the name Darkmover. "That's why I also got a GPS chip implanted."

Roger's eyes grow wide with surprise. "Seriously?"

I show him the underside of my left arm. I take off the small round band-aid between my shoulder and elbow, and all that can be seen of the device is a tiny red mark where it's been embedded under my skin. "It's about the size of a grain of rice. RFID. Essentially a small antenna in a tiny glass tube. A lot of wealthy people in Mexico afraid of being kidnapped have been using them as a precautionary measure."

"How does it track?"

"The chip sends a signal to an external GPS unit in this." I hold out my hand with a small circular disk. "I'll wear this in my bra. The chip also relays a signal to an external GPS device. Here." I hand Roger what looks like a small cellphone. He opens it and sees a green light pulsing. "In case… anything happens and the device is no longer on me… the system can track me down by sending radio pings to the implant."

I pause. "There are some minor issues. The chip only has about a week's worth of power before it would need a battery to recharge. If I'm away from a power source for more than seven days, it could be rendered useless. In addition, the range is limited, and thick metal or concrete walls can decrease the signal." I see that registering on Roger's face, which is quite glum. "But, hey, I guess all that talk about Bill Gates implanting microchips for medical and purchasing purposes is here. Maybe I can buy you a Starbucks with it," I quip.

A weak grin turns up Roger's mouth, but it disappears quickly. "We've got to be ready for everything. Are you sure you're up for this?"

"Rog, you're the one who said I do things because they're right, not because they're easy. And we'll have the FBI right behind us as soon as we have eyes on Darkmover." I pause. "And you? You good?"

He's wearing his producer "I've-got-this-covered" face. "We leave first thing in the morning."

Chapter 83

Instead of calling, Charles Wilcox texts flight and hotel information for TJ and Roger to Darkmover on their special secure line. It's acknowledged it with a happy face emoji.

I can't stand to hear that disgusting voice anymore. Soon I won't have to.

Steve Godfrey with NCI was more than happy to share the pair's information with him. *Talk about loose lips. That moron played right into my hands.*

Wilcox absentmindedly runs his hand over his thinning hair and blows out a pent-up sigh of relief. He knows that damned reporter will be out of his hair soon and he can go back to lining his Cayman bank account with the extra funds from his operation to help migrants "work" in this country.

Joining forces with Darkmover was a gamble on his part he'd thought would reap bigger benefits, but in the long run, it was not worth it, given the power Darkmover had begun to hold over him.

Will Darkmover let him off the hook? That remains to be seen.

Chapter 84

It's a 12-hour flight to Bucharest, with a change of planes and a three-hour layover in Paris.

"Maybe we can stay in France for a couple of days on the way back?" I suggest to Roger as we're stretched out in business class on Air France. "I'd love to go the Louvre again... or maybe check out the fountains in Aix-en-Provence?"

Roger gives me that "I can't believe you're talking about that" look.

"I know, I know. Gotta focus." I try to relax, but the whole operation has all my muscles as stiff as the wing on the jumbo jet. "Still, I can't remember the last time I took a vacation. I think we'll need one after this."

Roger smiles. "I like the 'we' sound of that." He gets a faraway look in his eyes. "It's been years since I was in Paris. And it was all a working trip." He looks at me again. "Let's not get too far ahead of ourselves, but... yes, that would be nice."

I smile back. Paris. The City of Love. I can see us sitting at a sidewalk café, drinking wine, sharing a baguette— *What the fuck, Banks!* I shake my head in disgust that my mind is wandering. "You're right. Can't think about that right now. Gotta keep my head in the game."

"Exactly. Let's go over the plan one more time." Roger pulls out his cell and opens his notes app. "At the airport, we'll meet with a former intelligence agent your friend Cho introduced me to and has worked with. He will also be our protection and translator..."

An overpowering feeling of doubt wears on me as we ride in a noisy taxi to the Bucharest hotel.

The quiver of butterflies in my stomach feels more like a colony of angry bees. I finger my necklace as I look out the vehicle's window.

"What is it?" Roger asks.

"Oh, just nerves, I guess."

"Look, if the slightest little thing doesn't feel right, we'll abort. No shame in that." Roger grasps my hand and gives it a squeeze.

I nod. "I just wish time would speed up a little bit."

"We'll check into the hotel, then get updates from everyone we have on the ground. We're not alone in this, you know. You've got Cho and her people, and the FBI will do the heavy lifting." He nods toward the front seat. "Plus, we've got Gabriel here who was with the Romanian Intelligence Service for more than a decade, going after traffickers, and is now one of the top cyber private investigators."

At the sound of his name, Gabriel, a tall, olive-skinned man with short military-cut hair, turns his head towards us. He dips his head in acknowledgement, and I notice his long black eyelashes surrounding his deep chocolate brown eyes.

"Right. I'm fine," I lie, as I shake out my hands. I blame the anxiety on my lousy recent track record of a bullet wound in my leg, the trafficker confronting me with a gun in my face and the high-speed chase and shooting near Sedona. *Will my luck change?*

Roger and I have adjoining rooms in a beautifully appointed hotel room in the heart of Bucharest's downtown area.

But I hardly notice the fresh flowers, king-sized bed and ornate drapery framing the tall windows.

Gabriel joins us in the sitting area, and we spread out maps and equipment.

"My group is an elite team of former agents, funded by the Romanian government. We have identified two locations where we believe Darkmover has been working," Gabriel says in a flawless Oxford English accent, a result, I learn, of his Westminster Boys School education. "We will send up a drone to the window of a high-rise building five blocks from here, where we believe the headquarters are." He points to the map. "The second is an operations room on the outskirts of the city. We arranged for a delivery there, and our man reported seeing a large screen on the wall that rolls up into a cylinder for travel. The dozen or so people work on laptops, which are plugged into half a dozen portable suitcase servers in padded metal shipping containers so the equipment can be quickly packed up and moved to the next location when needed."

"But where are the trafficked victims being held?"

"Those sites are not as readily apparent." Gabriel leans back in his chair. "But once we take down an operations room, we should be able to find potentially hundreds of locations."

"How certain are you these belong to Darkmover?"

"We are at 95% certainty. That's also why we need to move in the next day or so."

"I'll call Agent Porter." I stand, partially to quell the heavy feeling in my chest.

Chapter 85

"**I** wondered when you'd get here," Special Agent Aaron Porter says as he takes TJ's call.

It's nearly midnight in his small downtown Bucharest hotel room, hours after having tracked Darkmover to this capital city. His FBI team, partnering with local law enforcement, are prepared to move in and take them down.

"What? You're in Romania, too?" TJ exclaims, an incredulous tone in her voice.

"Guess we've both got good intel," Aaron says. "Look, I… I get it you're just trying to do the right thing. I'm willing to compare notes so this doesn't go south. Can we meet?"

Aaron hears TJ blow out a breath over the phone. *Relief? Anger?* He can't tell.

"Yes, of course. Now?"

He glances at his watch. "It's late, but sure." *Given her urgency, now he knows it's relief.* "Where?"

"We'll come to you."

"Who's we?"

"My producer, Roger Lester, and a local private cyber investigator, Gabriel. Where are you?"

Lester. Is he just a producer? Or is there more to that relationship? Aaron knows the two worked together years ago, and that she has been staying with him in Atlanta. He shakes his head. *Not important. Focus on the mission.*

Aaron gives her the address but admonishes her to be cautious. "Make sure your investigator watches for a tail. Take every precaution."

Chapter 86

Roger, Gabriel and I meet in Porter's cramped hotel room.

"Government budget," Aaron says apologetically.

It's awkward as hell for Roger and me to be sitting on the edge of Aaron's bed. The thought *I've slept with both these men* pings my brain. Aaron takes the desk chair, warily stealing glances at Roger, who wears his professional working face. Gabriel stands, pacing.

"We have identified a third potential location," Aaron says, his finger on the paper map. "But we agree the other two both our informants found are more likely the better targets."

"When can we move in?" I'm anxious to get going.

"There's that 'we' again." But with Aaron's smile, I get the feeling maybe he's not dissing me this time. "The FBI along with Gabriel and his people will set up two teams, one for each location. You will be in a safe location nearby. We will be in contact with you once we have accomplished the mission. Understood?"

I clench my teeth, as I feel the heat rise to my face. Part of me is ready to lash out at Aaron, while another part accepts his plan as the best one. "Fine."

Gabriel, who is next to the window, peers out through the closed curtains. "Our drone confirms they typically work under the cover of night. I suggest tomorrow, around midnight."

Aaron nods. "Agreed. Let's all get some sleep."

My eyes are heavy from fatigue and jetlag, but my nerves won't let slumber come.

I toss and turn in the hotel bed, snippets of scenes from the day whirling in my brain. Aaron, looking handsome in his white shirt with rolled-up sleeves, breath tinged with his ever-present mints, observing the interactions between Roger and me. Roger, playing it cool, but with a brief look of defeat as we were leaving. Gabriel, ever watchful, seemingly suspicious of everything and everyone.

I touch the implant in my arm. It's mostly healed, the small bandage is gone and only a tiny pink spot remains. But I can feel the small receptacle with my finger. *Hopefully I won't have to find out if it works.*

Gabriel, Roger and I drink strong espresso at a busy sidewalk café the next morning, down the street from where we believe Darkmover's operations center is.

One of Gabriel's people placed a tiny audio device on the heavily curtained outside window of the room in question, and it connects to an app on the investigator's cell phone. It lies open on the round metal table, and we all have earbuds Bluetoothed into it. Last night there was plenty of activity. But today there's no sound from the room, no physical activity detected coming or going.

Gabriel agrees to wear a small camera tonight so Roger and I can see and hear exactly what is happening.

"This location has a better opportunity for decent video than the office building." I take a sip of the robust coffee and look at Roger. "Is everything set up in the van?"

"Yes, for the fifth time. It will be across the street. We'll have audio and video monitors, and we can record from Gabriel's device. Your gear is all set up and ready to go, along with your Kevlar. I'll be wearing a vest as well and will be right beside you."

Gabriel sits with his legs stretched out, arms casually crossed, but behind his dark glasses, it's obvious his vigilant eyes are watching all around us.

"So, Gabriel, how long have you known about Darkmover?" I ask.

"About six to eight months," he replies, staying in his same position. "I've been working with Cho for a couple of years, and we had some intelligence about a large unidentified organization operating here. So, when she told me about your search, we were able to zero in and put a name to it."

"What other types of cyber investigations are you involved in?"

"Only sex trafficking."

Another person dedicated to fighting this horrific crime. "May I ask why?"

Gabriel's head slowly turns toward me. "My younger sister. She ran away from home when she was 15 and was lured into that world through social media. I lost contact with her a couple of years ago, but I'm still looking for her."

Like Katrina. I get a pang in my heart thinking of her. "I have a friend who I believe also fell into sex trafficking. I'm hunting for her, too."

Gabriel looks back down the street. "Only one in a hundred is rescued. But we must have hope. Maybe we will make it two."

Chapter 87

Roger and I are seated in the panel van by 10 p.m.

There's a detailed console with buttons and dials below three video monitors. One screen will show Gabriel's camera, and the other two will have footage from body-worn cameras on Aaron's FBI team members, one from the office location and the other from the operations center. There's barely enough room for two folding chairs.

I sit on one, but my knee nervously pops up and down and I can hardly keep my hands still. I check and recheck my camera, microphone, earphones.

"Relax, TJ." Roger is the epitome of calm, leaning back casually in his chair, arms behind his head. "Take a deep breath."

I do as he suggests. I close my eyes and feel my lungs expand and contract as I push the air in and out.

There's a knock on the van's back door. I jerk to attention.

Roger looks at his watch and gets up to let him in. "That'll be Gabriel."

But it's not Gabriel's face peering at us. I see Roger stiffen. "Who are you?" he demands.

"Apologies," whispers the stocky, muscular man with a dark growth of beard. "I replacing Gabriel," he continues in a heavy Romanian accent.

"Wait, I don't understand. Why? Where is he?" Roger asks.

"Not out here." The man pulls himself into the van. "That Covid virus. Gabriel test positive today. Must quarantine. He send me. Give me his gear." He points to the pen in his pocket, the same device we provided Gabriel earlier today, along with his small walkie-talkie.

"This is highly irregular," Roger looks at me, brows together, worry on his face.

"What did Gabriel tell you about the operation?" I share Roger's concern.

"Everyting I need to know. I vork vit heem for many years. Ees no problem."

He says his name is Marius, and he's worked with Gabriel in the Romanian Intelligence Service, or SRI, Serviciul Român de Informaţi.

I can tell Roger is not comfortable with the change, but he knows I don't want to abort the operation.

"Let me make a call," Roger says, stepping out of the van.

I go over the plans with Marius.

It's nearly midnight, and Aaron texts my cell:

Marius checks out. But watch him.

I text back: *TY. Ready?*

Aaron: *In position. Be ready.*

Me: *Standing by. Be careful.*

"Agent Porter and his team are in position." It's just Roger and me in the van, as Marius is already with the op center group. "He says they checked Marius out but to keep an eye on him." The video monitors flicker to life with dark jiggling motions as the agents creep toward the two targets.

Sweat drips under my Kevlar vest, even though the van's AC is on high. I set down the camera and wipe my damp hand for what feels like the 15th time. My post is by the door where I can watch the monitors and jump out the minute these sites are shut down to get footage of the traffickers being marched out in handcuffs.

"Go!" Aaron's voice shouts from one monitor, while Marius says the same on the other screen. Their footsteps pound the concrete and their breathing is heavy.

My eyes dart back and forth between the three images, and I think I recognize Aaron's muscular body leading Darkmover's office team. *Be safe. Don't get hurt.* A pang in my heart is evidence of the feelings I still have for him.

I glance at Roger, who is also watching the cameras intently. *He's more than a good friend, too. Stop. No time for those thoughts now.*

"I want to follow them." I grab my gear but stop at the door. I turn back to Roger. "Come with me?"

Roger's jaw clenches back and forth as he deliberates. "Okay, but we stay together."

I nod in affirmation.

We race out toward the building, my camera on a wide shot recording the officers in front of us. Marius and his group shout in Romanian, so I can't understand what they're saying. They breach the door, and their strong flashlights light up the room.

Which is empty.

The shouting stops. "What the hell?" I can't believe my camera's monitor.

With the exception of a few paper coffee cups, a couple of trashcans and some cables on the floor, the occupants have cleared out.

"Damn," says Roger, who's right beside me.

I text Aaron.

What hap

A strong arm roughly grabs my waist and a cloth presses hard against my mouth and nose. I try to twist around and catch a glimpse of Roger's wide eyes as another man in black has a rag over his face as well. A sweet smell like nail polish remover is all I remember.

Chapter 88

"TJ! Lester! Where the hell are you?"

FBI Agent Aaron Porter yells on his walkie-talkie but gets no response. He's stunned that his mission uncovered nothing in Darkmover's world other than some lavish office furniture. Initial reports from the other team also indicate a failed attempt at the operations center take-down.

We were so certain… how and when the hell did they get wind of us and manage to flee?

Porter tries again on the two-way comm system. "Marius, do you copy? Marius, this is Porter, come in." Again, nothing. "Marius, do you have the 20 for TJ and Lester? Do you cop—?"

Then over the small device comes a deep chuckle. "Go back vhere you come from, feebie," says a man's voice with a thick Romanian accent. "You no match for Darkmover."

Then static.

Porter presses the Talk switch a few times. "Who the hell are you?" he shouts. But there's no answer.

He whips out his cell phone. There's a moment of relief when he sees a text from TJ. But the sensation quickly turns to fear when he sees the partial message:

What hap

He calls TJ's cell, but it goes directly to voicemail.

"Luca! Ormerod!" Porter shouts to members of his team and motions for them to join him. The group of about a dozen law enforcement personnel gathers around him. "Two or three people from the other team may be missing. Someone from Darkmover's world may have intercepted Gabriel, and I can't reach the two media personnel. Luca, call your HQ and dispatch as many as possible to the other location. Ormerod, pick three from this group so we can head there A-sap."

Porter runs a hand over his face and head. He can feel it in his gut: something is very, very wrong.

By the time he arrives at the operations center, about 20 minutes later, Porter has tried TJ and Gabriel and Marius multiple times by phone, text and walkie, but to no avail.

He feels a brief glimmer of hope when he sees members of his team surrounding Roger Lester, who is sitting up on the ground, the white PRESS on his Kevlar glowing brightly in the dark night. "Lester! What the hell happened? Where's Banks?"

Lester holds his head with one hand as he looks up with dull eyes at the FBI agent. "I… we both… I think someone chloroformed us. I woke up here, but I don't know where TJ is."

"Fuck! Did anyone else see what happened? Where's the point man for this team? Where's Marius or Gabriel?"

A young man carrying a long rifle with "FBI" on his bulletproof vest steps forward. "We never saw Gabriel. Marius took his place at the last minute. He seemed to be familiar with the drill, so we continued the mission. When we didn't locate anyone inside and we exited the building, Marius had disappeared. We found the media guy here."

"God DAMN it." Porter shakes his head. He looks up and points to his group. "Okay, you five spread out and canvass the area. You're looking for a woman named TJ Banks, about 5 feet 9, short black hair, possibly still wearing a vest that says 'PRESS.' Luca, take two men and figure out what happened to Gabriel and see if you can find anything on this Marius."

Porter looks at Roger. "Lester, are you able to walk?"

Roger nods in the affirmative.

"Ormerod, help Lester into the van. We need to figure out what the hell is going on."

With that, Porter stamps across the street, leading the way to TJ and Lester's media vehicle.

Chapter 89

My cheek is cold and there's grit pressing into it.
Eyes flutter open to a black room that's cold and damp. *What the hell? Where am I?*

As I adjust to the darkness, I slowly pull myself up to a sitting position. I try to swallow, but my mouth is dry and it burns. That's when I remember the sweet-smelling cloth against my mouth during the attempt to take down one of Darkmover's locations.

I wipe the dirt and sand off my face and do a check of my body: my neck hurts, probably from lying in a strange position, but nothing else seems to be damaged. My Kevlar vest is gone, but I've still got my same clothes on.

Shit, where's Roger?

"Rog, are you here?" I try to look around the small enclosure, which appears to be a walled-off section of what might be a basement with a filthy concrete floor. A single wood door comes into focus. I crawl towards it, my head swimming with dizziness.

It's locked.

I sit against the wall beside it and try to get my brain to clear.

Have I been kidnapped? Roger, too? By Darkmover or Wilcox or both?

Marius. Taking Gabriel's place. *Is he a Darkmover mole? Did they get rid of Gabriel and intercept the operation?*

Gotta get out of here. But my head is still hazy, and I think I'm going to throw up.

I rattle the doorknob again, but it's locked tight. *Maybe I can take the hinges off.* I feel them with my fingers, but they're solid and unmoving. No windows in the dank space. My heart starts to beat faster, and it's uneven at times, which is probably from the chloroform used to knock me out.

Oh, shit! What am I going to do?

I can feel the panic trying to take over. Disgusting bile rises in my throat and I turn to the side and vomit onto the floor. The taste is repulsive, and I throw up again. I wipe my mouth with my shirtsleeve.

Where's Roger? Where's Aaron? They'll find me, right? But what do I do in the—

Footsteps. Coming to the door. I slowly stand, hiding behind the door although waves of vertigo and nausea almost force me back down.

The door opens and a man in dark clothing enters, looking around, his hand still on the knob. *Can I remember the restraint training I took years ago?* When I first started investigating sex trafficking, I wanted to make sure I could defend myself in a crisis situation if needed. I remember my instructor, a former wrestler named Tony, saying the biggest problem in control tactics is that people try to exert control too soon. *I don't have a choice.*

I jerk back on the door, and thrust my left leg out, which trips the man. He goes to the floor with a grunt. With my foggy head, I don't move fast enough to catch him while he's down, and he rolls over and snaps back up. He grabs my arm and twists it so hard I think it's going to break.

Things start to go black, but I remember another Tony line: *Stay upright to survive!* I shake my head to stay conscious and turn back around toward my attacker, who yanks my wrist. I go with the pull toward him, locking my body against his and trapping his arms. I pull straight up, twist him into the air and around and throw him to the ground.

Run! I race out of the room. There's a set of wooden stairs. I run up the dozen or so steps and hesitate at the top, where there's a closed door. I turn the knob quietly and open it a couple of inches to peek out. No one.

I'm in a kitchen on the first floor of what looks like an older residential home. Ancient stove, oven, refrigerator, dark brown cabinets and shelves. Still dark outside. A back door. I make a dash for it as I hear footsteps thump up the stairs behind me from the basement.

I push the door outwards and another man, dressed in dark green, has his back to me, possibly standing guard. I lunge for his shoulders and wrap my right arm around his neck. I get a chokehold on him when the other attacker grabs me from behind. Between the two of them, I'm overpowered. I go limp.

"Fuckin' beetch." A Romanian accent from the first attacker, who grabs my ankles while the guard takes my wrists. They carry me back through the kitchen and down the stairs, my back scraping painfully against the steps. They toss me like a bag of potatoes on the floor, where I roll once and land on my side.

"You need to learn lesson." The original attacker walks over and kicks my stomach hard with his boot. "Uuggh!" I scream. The pain is fierce. He kicks again. This time I let go of consciousness and black takes over.

Chapter 90

Roger Lester's head pounds as he guzzles a bottle of water inside the van.

The cool liquid helps the burning in his throat, but the brain fog is incapacitating. *What happened? How did we get attacked? Where did they take TJ?*

Roger blinks his eyes several times, but they won't focus. He closes them and tries to answer the questions Agent Porter shouts at him. "I think… it was two men. I remember seeing someone dressed in… a dark shirt and pants with his hand clamping a cloth over TJ's mouth. About the same time it was happening to me."

"What the hell happened to Gabriel? And who is this Marius?" Porter paces back and forth inside the small vehicle.

I can see where HIS priority is, and it's not T—.

"Never mind that," Porter interrupts. "We gotta find Banks." He whips out his cell phone.

"Wait a minute." Roger sits up, his head clearing a bit. "We have a way… I mean we have a couple… Hold on…" He fumbles in his pockets.

Porter turns to him. "What are you talking about?"

Roger rubs his eyes. "My phone." He reaches into his pocket and retrieves his cell. "Earrings… I gave her earrings…" His eyes have trouble focusing on the phone's screen and his fingers don't want to cooperate.

"Why the fuck are you talking about some gift at a time like this?"

Roger glares at Porter. "It's not what you think. It's for tracking… there's a… microchip behind each stone. Here, open this app, my eyes are too fuzzy."

He hands the cell to Porter, who nimbly engages the software and starts tapping.

"Do you see her?" Roger asks.

"Not yet." Porter widens the search area on the phone with his fingers.

"She… TJ also had… an RFID device implanted in her arm."

Porter looks at Roger, his eyes wide. "No shit." He shakes his head. "That woman…" he trails off.

You condescending bastard. "That woman is smart and tough." Roger stands up, still shaky on his feet. "She had a bad feeling this whole time, so she wanted to be prepared." He pulls out and opens the device TJ had given him. "This is the implant's GPS tracker, but I don't see anything yet. I think we're too far away."

Porter gives him a look that's part grimace and part like he's about to shed a tear.

Shit, is Porter in love with her? Roger's heart sinks momentarily, but then he realizes: *She may not be in love with him.*

A "ding" sounds from Roger's phone, still in Porter's hand. Porter looks down, then turns it toward Roger. A round red light is blinking on and off from the chip in the earrings.

"There she is." Porter nods.

Chapter 91

This time, I wake with a start.

I'm curled up on the same dirty floor as before. My arms are in front of me, wrists secured together with something tight. My stomach throbs. Once again, I'm alone in the room. It's pitch black.

I gingerly push myself up on one elbow, and the muscles in my back complain loudly.

How am I going to get out of here? A feeling of dread comes over me. *WILL I get out of here?*

My hands go to my ears and touch Roger's earrings with the chip, then reach into my bra and feel the GPS device. I blow out a breath of relief. *I've got both devices. He'll find me! It'll be all right.*

I ease back down on my side and try to relax, even though my body aches.

"Be careful." So many people warned me. A tear drips from my eye. *And what did I do? Disregard them? Disregard my safety? For what? A TV story? A great clip of video?*

No. I'm trying to save lives. I'm trying to stop the scum who are destroying the futures of women, boys and girls.

A renewed energy comes over me. *I can't wait around until they rescue me. I need to do something. I have to be ready.*

I slowly pick myself up. The constraint training comes back to me in bits and pieces. The primary way kidnappers restrain their victims is with duct tape, and that's exactly what they've done with me. I can't see my wrists in the darkness, but with a couple of fingers I feel the smooth surface, and it's wound tight. I remember one of the first things Tony taught us: how to break duct tape bindings.

We were all amazed when he simply raised his hands above his head, then quickly pulled his arms down on either side of him. Sure enough, soon we were all able to get out of the restraints.

I bring my arms up toward the ceiling, then I yank them down fast, as if I'm trying to slap my hips. Instead, my back and stomach register fierce pain. No good. I take a couple of breaths and try again. I jerk hard and miraculously, it works.

I leave the tape dangling from my wrists, in case I need to pretend I'm still bound.

I gingerly raise myself to an upright position. I shake off some dizziness and take deep breaths to calm myself.

I find the door and pound on it. "Hey!" It comes out as a squeak. I clear my throat and try again.

"What the hell do you guys want from me? Come show yourselves!"

I listen. Nothing. I try the door again. Locked tight. I feel around the walls with my hands and swipe the floor with my feet to see if I can find anything to use to protect myself.

I knock something with my shoe and it skitters across the floor. I follow the sound in the darkness and go down on my hands and knees, patting the concrete until I locate a small piece of rough wood about five inches long, and thin. *Maybe a tree branch of some kind?*

I sit with my back to the wall and run it around in my fingers. Holding the end at an angle against the floor, I scrape and scrape the end into a point, hoping to make it a weapon. When I hear voices from outside, I hide the stick in my fist.

I stand up, back against the wall, hands together as if still taped, and wait as the door opens. As my eyes adjust to the light outside, two men stand in silhouette. *Not good odds. For anyone.* My heart beats faster.

"*Ai grija. Ca e gata,*" says the shorter one, who called me a bitch before.

"He says you feisty?" The taller one enters the room, something long and thick in his hand. "Ve show you vhat vee do vith feisty girls." He walks cautiously toward me, the baton in his hand coming into my view.

"No, guys, look, it's not like that. I don't have a clue what you want with me, but there will be a cavalry of FBI agents and other cops who will be here very soon." I inch into the far corner. "I'm a journalist, and you can go away for a long time for kidnapping me. But if you just let me go, we—"

"Shut up!" The men take positions on either side of me. The one with the baton raises his hand and swings it down hard on my shoulder.

"No!" I scream, recoiling against the wall.

Chapter 92

The man strikes me again, this time on my raised forearm.

The pain is sharp and the blow renders my hand numb for a few moments.

I do my best to recover and thrust my right leg out against the short man, connecting with his kneecap, which forces him to the ground. The tall guy comes toward me again, but before he can raise his weapon, I stab the stick hard into his chin. He drops the baton and clutches his face as I make a beeline for the open door. This time I shut the door and turn the deadbolt into the locked position from the other side.

Once again, I scramble up the stairs and out into the kitchen, where the sun is up, casting early morning shadows on the tall leafy trees outside.

I take my chances on finding another way out, this time perhaps through something other than a guarded door. In the small living room, a turquoise sofa with doilies on the arms sits in front of two windows. I try to raise the wood frame, but my shoulder stings with pain and I can't get it to budge. The feeling is back in my hand, so I grab a wooden chair sitting at a dining room table and smash it through the glass. I throw the chair to the ground and am going to dive through the window when I hear a female Romanian voice say, "Stop right there!"

I freeze when I see a tall woman calmly pointing a pistol at me. She's maybe in her 40s, lean with well-defined arms showing through a short-sleeved, loosely fitting dress. Her chestnut hair is pulled back severely from her face into a low, tight bun. She reminds me of a ballerina.

I put my hands up. "Don't shoot." *I could take her if she didn't have a gun. Where the hell are Roger and Aaron? Now what do I do?*

"You haf not been a veddy nice guest." The woman walks slowly around the sofa, still aiming the weapon toward me.

"Guest? Do you tie up all your guests and throw them down in your basement?"

She chuckles. "Only zee vons who need to learn acceptance."

One of the two men I locked in the basement, a beefy guy with a big gut, appears in the living room with two more guys. One is short and stocky, but with huge biceps, like a wrestler, and the other is skinny and wiry. "Take her upstairs. Perhaps a bed vill help her be more cooperative." She nods to her goons.

"You don't want to do this. There are people coming for me. They're close."

"No von is comink vor you, my dear." The woman studies me from head to toe and back up again. "And she looks veddy uncomfortable in all dose clothes."

The trio overpowers me, lifting me off the floor. "No! Leave me alone!" I try to fight them off, but the three are much too strong.

They carry me up a narrow stairwell to a room with only a small four poster double bed in it. No dressers, no chairs, no pictures on the wall. A filthy mattress. One small window, no drapes.

I do everything I can to wrench out of their grip, but I wear myself out, and my body pulses with pain. While Wrestler and Fat Gut hold me on the smelly bed, Wiry Guy ties my arms and ankles with rope to the four corners of the wooden frame. The first two take off my shoes and socks and toss them on the floor.

Wiry Guy draws a long pair of sharp scissors from his back pants pocket.

Oh, god, is he going to stab me? I'll bleed out right here!

"No! Please! Don't hurt me!"

But he takes the scissors and slowly, carefully, almost seductively cuts off my jeans and my shirt, leaving me in only my bra and panties. He also removes my earrings, his rough hands struggling to pull the tiny backs from the posts, and puts them in his pocket. *Oh, no, the tracking device! But I've still got the implant.*

"Who are you? What do you want with me?" I shriek.

The Fat Gut guy, who has an old scar running down his cheek, grabs my breast and squeezes tight. I wince. His breath stinks of coffee and booze, and his shirt, unbuttoned too far at the top, exposes graying chest hair. "You vill find out soon enough." They all laugh and leave the room.

Oh, god, what have I done?

Chapter 93

Steven Godfrey frantically paces back and forth in front of the black night-time windows in his office at NCI, dots of light sprinkling from downtown D.C. buildings.

Dark circles of concern and lack of sleeplessness ring his eyes. His wrinkled polo shirt and the casual blue jeans are not his typical office wear. The cell in his hand rings and he punches a key.

"What the fuck is going on, Wilcox?" he snaps. "Where is TJ?"

"Why, whatever are you talking about?" replies Charles Wilcox, too calmly.

"You goddamn better know! TJ Banks is missing. Her team thinks she's been kidnapped. I trusted you and your information. How did this happen?"

"Calm down, Godfrey. I gave you a lead on a sex trafficking organization in Europe. That's where my role ends."

"No way, you bastard. You assured me your info was legit and that you would have people to move in to assist TJ and her producer."

"It appears the FBI is already involved, so I let them take the lead."

"You sonofabitch, if I find out you had some—"

"Now look here, Godfrey," Wilcox interrupts. "This Darkmover is very strong and powerful. You and Ms. Banks should have known there was danger involved. This is no longer my concern."

"The hell it isn't!" Godfrey screams. "You—"

But the line is dead.

Charles Wilcox smiles with a sigh of relief.

He locks his burner phone back in the center drawer of his office desk. *Banks is out of my way, Darkmover has a new toy, and all is right with the world.*

But then Darkmover's voice haunts his brain with "a swarm of gnats can be aggravating and irritating" and the line about not wanting him "missing fingers or hands." He rubs his mouth nervously.

No, he must be very careful, as he always is. His security detail, standing outside his door in Washington, D.C. at this very moment, will protect him against Darkmover's thugs.

He hopes.

Chapter 94

Sharp pain emanates from my shoulder, my arm, my back.

There are muffled sounds of movement from downstairs, but I can't distinguish voices.

It's bloody hot and still in this room, and my arms or legs are immobile. I can move my head back and forth slightly, and can shift my butt, but only an inch or two in either direction. Not enough to help me out of these bindings, which are tight and cutting into my skin.

A fly buzzes at the dirty second-floor window. You're trapped too, eh, buddy? It bangs against the glass time and again. *I know the feeling. At least you've got your wings. Not that you're going to break through that barrier.*

How am I going to get out of here?!

The implant! I turn my head and there it is. The tiny spot, barely visible, on my left arm. I can only hope the disc is still inside my bra. I close my eyes in relief.

Oh, god, please Roger, please Aaron, open the app and find me!

How long have I been here? How long was I out from the chloroform? It's probably been at least 24 hours. It could be more. And the charge on the implant only lasts seven days …

My eyes pop open again and adrenaline spikes. *What if it doesn't work? What if the battery's dead already? What if they don't find me? What are these people going to do to me?*

Stop panicking and think! These must be cohorts of Darkmover, that slimy bastard who treats women and children like sex slaves.

Oh god! Will they try that with me? There's no way I would let… The thought nauseates me. *But will I have a choice? Did the other women have a choice?*

My thoughts go back to the years of research I've done and the many victims I've interviewed. For many it starts off when an older man grooms a young woman, often a runaway or someone with low self-esteem who gets in with a bad crowd. The women are promised a high-paying job, fancy clothes and shoes and a loving relationship. Many believe that man is their boyfriend and they fall in love.

One woman was told all she had to do was "give somebody a massage." She thought that didn't sound so bad. But she had no idea it would become her everyday lifestyle to be forced into sex.

Another woman, Sylvia, was told she had to "do her part" to earn her keep in exchange for food, clothes and a place to sleep. For her, it eventually became normalized and seemed safer than being on the streets. But she was repeatedly raped and forced to meet a $500-a-night quota. When she didn't, she was beaten.

The pain in my stomach from being kicked is a reminder of how helpless women and children can become.

I'm not weak nor helpless! Or am I? I'm tied up and locked in this room. They're going to beat me and rape me and god knows…

Stop! Don't go there. That's not going to help.

But my mind goes back to the girls who refuse sex or try to escape, and the stories of traffickers using physical and psychological violence and drugs to control them. Angelique's traffickers got her hooked on heroin, and she did their bidding in order to feed her habit. Other new "recruits" realize too late the full reality of their new situation, and readily available drugs help numb their pain and endure the rapes.

One woman, who had been trafficked from her teens to her late 20s, told me, "First you need to escape your own mind, right?"

That was a common theme: to go to another place in their minds, to disassociate, to get through the nightmare.

With all these thoughts running through my mind, I finally understand how many young women would simply give up and just do as they're told to avoid pain.

But I wouldn't do that—would I? Is it inevitable? Do you get so low you don't believe there's any way out? Is there no way out for me?

Chapter 95

Oh, god, what did I do to get myself into this position?!
I thought I was doing the right thing. Helping women and children. Exposing the scum of the earth, getting them behind bars.

Did I let down my guard? Was I distracted by all those thoughts about Aaron and Roger and Michael and settling down somewhere? That must be it. I was preoccupied with visions of my own place, a full-time steady job, all the shiny things Steve Godfrey from NCI was promising me that I lost my focus. Got sidetracked and wasn't paying attention to the mission.

I'm not a religious person, but suddenly I'm bargaining for help with a very unfamiliar entity some call God. *If you get me out of here, I'll…* I'll what? Find religion? Swear off men? Forget settling down and keep my nomadic life? Or settle down and dump the nomadic life? *I have nothing with which to make a deal. I've tossed losing dice. My chips are gone. There's noth—*

Steps approach the door and it opens. The same tall ballerina-like woman enters, no gun this time. She smiles, a sickeningly sweet grin.

I pull at my restraints, the pain sharp on my skin. "Let me go! Who are you? What do you want with me?"

"Ve'll take zee last question first," she says calmly. "Ees simple. Vee vant you to stop meddling in our business." She looks me over from top to bottom. "And vee haf successfully accomplished that."

"I am a journalist. There are people out there who are looking for me. And when they find me, they will take you—"

"*Eef* they are looking, they veel not find you. Besides, I think they have given up by now. Zee sooner you realize that, zee better it vill be for you and zee sooner you can adjust to your new life here."

"New life? Are you fucking kidding me? Who the hell do you think you are?"

"Ahh yes, zee first question. My name ees Ileana Barrionuevo. I believe you know me as Darkmover."

I'm stunned. *What?! No way, that can't be! My brain can't process that. A woman? All along we thought Darkmover was a man and it's a goddamn woman?*

"You?! But all this time… why… how… how can you treat women and children like sex slaves?"

The woman chuckles and shakes her head. "No, no, you have eet all wrong. Zey are part of our family. I give zem food, clothing, medical treatment, education, a day off. You are a part of our family now, too. And you vill command a high price."

"That's bullshit! There's no way—"

"Zee sooner you accept your new life, the easier eet vill be. Like zee others, you vill learn when you respect your family, vee treat you like family."

"I will never—"

"Oh, yes, you vill." Darkmover's eyes go black and her smile is gone. "Because zees is our business. I grew up in zee family business, and I survived and have made it very profitable for many. I treat our family much better than I was treated as a child…" She stops. Smiles that sick smile again. "Ees vhat I am very familiar with. And now vee like Realtors: vee expert at moving our family to new locations. 'New home, new adventure,' I like to say. Een zee next day or two, you vill go to a new home where you vill—"

"You goddamn fucking sonofabitch, you—"

Illeana / Darkmover strides to the bed and slaps me hard across the face. "Vee do not speak zat way to our family."

"I will *never* be part of your fucking—"

She slaps me again. Harder still.

My face stings and tears well up, but I'm not going to cry in front of this witch.

"Vee haf other vays to help you understand zat zees ees for zee best." Her hand goes into a pocket and she draws out a small syringe. She takes off the tip, puts it up to the light and pushes the plunger so a few drops come out the top.

"No! Please, don't!"

She injects my arm with whatever is in the needle.

"Zees will also help you realize you need to contribute to zee family."

My eyes get heavy and despite my blurry vision, Darkmover smiles again and heads for the door. As the door opens and closes, I feel my body slump and all goes dark.

Chapter 96

"It looks like a farmhouse in the Czech Republic, on the outskirts of Jablonec, about two hours northeast of Prague."

FBI Agent Aaron Porter is in a utilitarian Romanian Interpol office in Bucharest with Roger Lester and other team members from the failed busts of Darkmover's locations. They gather around a map on a large computer screen where two faint red lights are blinking.

"Interpol is gathering people on the ground there. We leave in an hour to fly to Prague, then will take vehicles from there."

"Can't you get anybody into the house sooner?" Roger Lester gestures at the map. "God knows what they're doing to TJ."

Porter clenches his jaw. He pushes the horrifying images from his brain that he assumes Lester is imagining as well. "Look, we are doing the best we can. We both want the same thing here."

"I know, I know." Lester rubs his eyes. "What else can NCI and I do?"

"Do NOT send any of your TV people to the site, is that clear?" Porter's voice goes up a notch in volume. "The last thing we need are—"

"We NEED to move faster!" Roger stands abruptly. "Darkmover and his people... they're ruthless. And they're five steps ahead of us at every move."

Porter knows he's right. And he fears the worst for TJ. "Look, the FBI has a long-standing partnership with Romania, but we don't have law enforcement authority here. We're going into some remote areas... so just make certain the tracking apps are online and working." He looks around the room. "That goes for everyone. We need to make sure we have plenty of battery power, satellite access and working internet as we go into these areas that probably won't have good, if any, service."

Roger looks at his phone, which is hooked up to a battery station on the desk. "I'm fully charged and ready to go."

Porter nods. "Is there anything from TJ's hotel room that would be of use?"

Roger considers this. "I don't think so. I have all the gear with me. It would just be her personal items. I'll arrange to have it packed up."

Porter nods. "Do it, then let's go."

Chapter 97

It's so cold.

Where's a blanket? I can't reach—

My eyes fly open. It's dark and cold and I'm shivering. Pain. All over. I'm groggy and vaguely comprehend where I am: tied up to a bed in one of many of Darkmover's sex-trafficking houses.

My head is fuzzy as I try to recall the last thing I remember. Darkmover. Slapping me. The needle.

My shoulder, my arm throb with pain. As does my vagina.

I glance down to realize I am covered with bruises. And I am naked.

No. Not that. Please God.

I don't remember anything after Darkmover injected me with what could've been a date-rape type drug such as Rohypnol or Ketamine. I've never had personal experience with it before, but as I understand from stories I've done, it quickly leads to loss of consciousness and amnesia.

But the pain in my stomach and private parts tells me what probably happened: At least one of Darkmover's goons had his way with me.

And I could do nothing about it.

Tears flow as sobs wrack my battered body.

Now I understand.

How so many women and children can get swept into the world of coerced sex for money.

Most are groomed for this life and ease into it gradually. Few are kidnapped as I was. But the result is the same. They—make that we—are forced to have sex whether under the threat of pain, *fear or drugs.*

I can't believe I let this happen. I was an idiot. I didn't listen. To Cho, to Aaron, to Roger. "Be careful," they all said.

But I'm TJ Banks! I'm invincible! I'm the girl wonder, snuffing out traffickers one bust at a time!

What a fool I've been.

Tears of humiliation, regret, sorrow stream down my face, through my hair, onto the mattress under me. I was too busy seeking the next great piece of video, the next confirmation that a few more girls might have been saved by their captors—but were they? Did another one of Darkmover's groups close in to take their places? Did they whisk the victims off to yet another hiding place, where the abuse starts all over again? Is it a never-ending cycle?

A cycle in which one stubborn, selfish, egotistical idiot thought she could make a dent. Of course, I wasn't going to stop sex trafficking all together, but if I saved one woman, one little child, it would all be worth it, right? *Wrong.*

Because it led me here.

I get a dull pain in my chest when I realize neither tracking device worked, or I would've been rescued by now. I've lost track of how many hours or days it's been now.

I tug at the bindings around my wrists, my ankles. The rough ropes just scrape my skin and dig deeper into my flesh.

It's useless.

This is what I get.

"Vake up. Time to go."

The early morning light is a weak yellow, barely visible through the single window. Wrestler and Fat Gut are back, one untying the ropes around my arms and legs, and the other holding a gun on me.

"Don't try anyting stupid." Fat Gut jiggles the weapon for emphasis as he tosses a wad of fabric at me.

"Where are we going?" Painfully I sit up for the first time in however long and rub my aching wrists.

"Shut up. Get dressed."

My whole body is sore with every move, but I manage to get the baggy shift over my head. Wrestler snaps handcuffs on my arms and pulls me to my feet. A wave of dizziness hits me. The two men grab me by each arm and practically drag me out of the room.

"Darkmover's not going to say goodbye?" I quip.

"I said, shut up!"

There's a warm glow while the sun inches its way over the horizon as the goons toss me into the back of an old, grimy white van. They secure my handcuffs to another pair that's attached to a solid metal ring on the floor. There's no bench, so I slide down to the dirty surface and curl up as best I can, grateful to bend my arms and legs again.

"I vant to vish you safe travels." Darkmover's voice comes from the back of the van. "I vill see you in a couple of days."

"Where are you taking me?" I lift my head in her direction.

She steps into the vehicle, again with a syringe in her hand.

My heart thumps at the sight. "No, you don't have to do that. I'll be… I won't…"

"Ahh, but you need to prove to me you can be trusted."

"I can, really—"

"Let's hope so. Until then…"

She jabs me with the needle and smiles. My eyes get heavy as she leaves the van and the engine starts. The bumpy road makes every muscle hurt more. I pass out again.

Chapter 98

Roger Lester stares out the window of a back seat of a Mercedes Benz transport vehicle, speeding down the E-65 freeway, barely cognizant of the bright yellow fields of canola for oil whizzing by.

Agent Porter is up front, speaking quietly with another FBI man. A dozen more local and Bureau law enforcement personnel are also in the van, heading toward the blinking lights and hoping to rescue TJ.

Roger gets a nauseating feeling in his gut. "Porter. What if TJ isn't there?"

"We're following the tracking devices. That's all we have to go on at the moment."

Roger looks down at his apps for what seems like the millionth time. "Shit!"

"What?" asks Porter.

"I'm only seeing one device!"

It takes nearly six hours, but Aaron Porter, Lester and his team finally make it to the Jablonec farmhouse to search for TJ.

They've been following the one blinking tracking device from the earrings Lester gave her to wear, as there's been no connection to the implant in her arm. Porter feels a tightness in his chest with that loss, and he's sure Lester is dealing with similar emotions.

Porter makes sure Lester stays beside the vehicle while the law enforcement personnel approach the old wood structure, its paint peeling, surrounded by green fields and a few trees. Roger videotapes the scene from the vehicle.

But there are no cars, no movement outside or in.

Aaron Porter is fearful, not of what they'll find, but of what they won't find.

They storm through the doors, search every room, the basement, the second story. And come up empty-handed.

Not again! His men are as incredulous as they walk out dejected. Aaron exits and looks toward Roger Lester, camera to his eye. Aaron shakes his head, feeling sick to his stomach.

"We found the earrings." Aaron holds them out in his hand toward Lester, who takes them gingerly. "They were on a windowsill of one of the rooms that looked like an office. Appears they were here maybe two to three hours ago. A kettle on the stove was still warm. Any luck on the other device?"

Lester puts down the camera and tries the implant device app again. Nothing.

"No. Company says it could be the battery, could be no service, or that she's inside some secure vehicle or building. Goddamn it, now what?"

Chapter 99

It's hot and steamy, like a humid day in the Florida panhandle where my parents live.

They're both coming to greet me, all smiles, arms outstretched. It's so good to see them! It's been a long time. I've missed them. As I start to hug my mother, I'm suddenly jerked awake by rough hands.

"What…? Where …?"

"Shut up!" It's Fat Gut again, with his gun out, as Wrestler unlocks the metal cuffs and pulls me across the rough floor to the open doors of the van. My heels scrape in pain and finally land on the ground outside.

The bright sun blinds me, and the heat is scorching. I manage to get my feet working under me as they pull me toward what looks like a one-story concrete warehouse. *Where the hell am I? What is that smell? Like sewage and shit. Concentrate! Look around you. Red roofs. Barbed wire fence all around. Farmland beyond?*

It's only slightly cooler inside the building as my eyes adjust to the darkness. Other voices, male and female, in indistinct conversations. Faint music somewhere.

"Irene!" Fat Gut yells out as he yanks me down the hall.

A stocky woman with long straggly hair wearing a flowered dress and holding a clipboard saunters up. She looks me over from top to bottom. "Take her to number seven," she snarls in an unplaceable European accent to a couple of rough-looking men. "You, DeChantal! Get her cleaned up!"

"All right." Another woman, prettier, better dressed, joins Darkmover's thugs to take me down a hallway of doors on either side to a small room, again with only a bed inside.

I'm still a little woozy from the drugs, and despite being cuffed to the bed by one hand, I collapse on the mattress, this time with a reasonably clean fitted sheet. *Be glad for small things.*

"Be careful of zees one. She still learning to behave," Fat Gut says. With that, the two men leave me with deChantal.

"You've got to help me get out of here!" I whisper loudly to the woman. She stands by the closed door, her hands clasped in front of her, a pink robe with a tight belt accentuating a small waist and large breasts. Her blonde curls jiggle as she chuckles.

"Oh, now, don't talk that way. You'll get used to it."

An American! Thank goodness!

"Are you from the U.S. too? Oh, thank god! I'm TJ. Look, where are we? I've got people coming for me. I'm sure they'll be—"

She laughs. "Right, honey, that's what they all say. Look, the sooner you go along with the routine, the better off you'll be. And yeah, I'm from Alabama and I'm really Cheryl. But they give all the girls new sexier names."

"But I don't—"

"Let me take a look at you. About size 10, I think? What color do ya like? I'll pick out a nice robe and come back to help you with a spit bath—"

"What are you doing? How can you… Are you here of your own free will?"

"Oh, no, but I learned a long time ago to go with the flow. It's sure better than the alternative." She looks off, the pleasantness on her face fading with some distant memory. Her head snaps back up again and she smiles. "Hey, this place isn't so bad. The food's decent, they buy us nice clothes, we get to travel to different places… They even make the clientele take showers before they can be with us."

I'm dumbfounded into silence.

"I'll be right back." She flashes me a cheery grin and leaves. The door locks behind her.

I lie back on the bed. I'm still sore all over, but now my mind reels. *They've brainwashed the women to do their evil bidding. I'll never get out of here…*

Chapter 100

Cheryl/deChantal returns shortly with a cheap, bright red satin cover-up as well as a metal bowl of tepid water and an old, worn washcloth.

She's accompanied by one of the thugs carrying a handcuff key, who unlocks my restraint so I can bathe. Silently, turning from his gaze as much as possible, I wash the top half of my aching body, then Cheryl gently scrubs the grime from my feet and knees, pulling out a few splinters from my heels.

"I need to… go to the bathroom." *Maybe that would give me a chance to escape.*

The man kicks a bucket from the corner of the room toward me. "Go," he says brusquely.

The thought of peeing in front of both of them almost makes me want to hold it longer. But I desperately need to relieve myself. I squat over the pail. When I'm done, I wipe with the wet cloth, my vagina still sore. The man leaves, closing the door behind him.

I trade the shift for the red robe and sit on the edge of the bed, rubbing my wrists. "Don't you want to get out of here and go home?"

Cheryl points to a tiny camera in the top corner of the room. "They can hear and see everything." She lowers her voice. "Yeah, it's hard at first, but the sooner you do as they say, the less painful it will be for you." She picks up the bowl and the old shift. "Oh, and I heard them say your new name will be Veronica. See you around."

What the fuck? I follow behind her as she opens the door. "Look, you can do what you want, but I've got to get outta here." With that, I push her aside, and run out of the room.

Straight into the arms of Wrestler.

I fight with all I have, which turns out to be not much.

In the end, it takes Wrestler, Fat Gut and some other goon to force me back into the small room and tie me up to the bedposts once again.

Only this time I'm on my stomach.

"Please, don't do this!" I beg.

"You vill learn," Fat Gut snarls. "How you say een America? 'Zee hard way.'" The three men chuckle.

I feel the sharp sting of something as it whips me on my back. "Noooo!"

One of the men hits me again and again, each snap loud in my ear as well as instant pain on my skin. Then warmth, as I imagine blood, seeps from the open wounds. I'm about to pass out from the pain, when the beating stops and they untie me, flip me over and retie the ropes.

A new burning sensation from my bleeding skin as it hits the sheet. "Aaagh!" I scream in agony.

Fat Gut is holding a short black leather crop, like those used for training horses. He slaps it against his hand, an evil grin on his ugly face.

I let the blackness of the pain take over.

I've always been strong, stubborn. Like my horoscope sign, Taurus the Bull.

But now I feel beaten down to the core. Powerless. Hollowed out.

I keep my eyes closed, knowing that when I open them, I will face the reality of my situation.

And I finally realize how women, especially children, get trapped in this life. You'll do about anything to minimize the pain, whether from beatings or drugs. "Go with the flow. Do what they say."

I can't believe they've broken me. I've had to surrender, yield to their force and their every whim. A tear rolls down the side of my face.

I dare to open my eyes. In the room it's dark, silent, but I can hear distant voices outside.

Is that a scream? A woman. Hurting. Fearful.

What did Roger tell me? That I later repeated to Aaron?

"You're fearless. Because it's right, not because it's easy."

Don't give up! And don't give in. Don't give them that power. Damn it, TJ, you are better than this!

Remember the mission. Must keep going, no matter what. Be fearless.

Chapter 101

Agent Aaron Porter, Roger Lester and a few members from the Europol team return to a dull gray Prague to regroup.

Still no sign of TJ's implanted device on the tracking software. And it's day five on its battery.

Porter knows the first 24 hours in any kidnapping case are critical, and his chest is tight knowing at four days since she was taken, it's way beyond that. And they have nothing.

Roger Lester paces the terrazzo floor of the Europol office, recovered from being chloroformed, but looking drawn and dejected.

"Lester, can you contact TJ's cyber friend, Cho? See if she has anything?"

Lester stops to look out the window at the dreary day and nods. "Already have. She is working her contacts hard. I've got the implant manufacturer trying to see if there's anything else they can do to get the signal working again." Roger turns to glare at Aaron. "And what are *you* doing to find TJ?"

Porter bites his tongue against a sharp retort. "I have our Homeland Security working the airports from Europe to the United States, and Europol is checking other mass transportation here. But if they moved her in a regular vehicle, it will be next to impossible to…" His voice trails off.

"She can't just disappear! Someone has to know some—"

Porter's cell phone interrupts Lester's diatribe, and he puts it to his ear. "Porter." He listens a moment, then drops his head. "Where?" He shakes his head at the voice on the line. "Got it. Thanks." He clicks off the call. "They found Gabriel."

Lester looks up in anticipation. "Is he okay? What happened?"

"No. He's dead. They found him shot in the head about three miles from the operations center. A professional hit."

Lester runs his hand angrily through his hair. "God *damn* it, I never should've let that Marius take over. What the hell was I thinking? I should've—"

"Lester, you had no way of knowing. My team checked him out and didn't suspect either."

"So, the only other person who might have any idea of what happened is gone." Roger paces a few more steps, then halts, an idea appearing on his face. "Look, we need to go live with this. Get the news out to all the major media—"

"No way!" Porter interjects. "That is not a—"

"Yes! The more people who know about it, the better chance we have of someone coming forward who has seen something. NCI will give a large reward and someone will talk."

"Hold on, I—"

"No, *you* hold on. We are getting nowhere, and we have to move faster. Until Cho comes up with something, I'm moving forward with this. And *you've* gotta be on board. You'll have to make a statement." His eyes soften, pain showing behind them. "For TJ."

Porter blows out a breath. He knows they must do whatever is necessary. And it just might work… "Okay, fine. Tell me what you need."

Chapter 102

Minutes later, Roger Lester has a small camera on a tripod set up in the room, with transmitting equipment attached and working.

While the other operatives murmur in low tones, working their computers and phones, he's been on his cell with Steve Godfrey at NCI, waiting to break into the current programming on CNN and other major U.S. networks. NCI also has alerted BBC and other international media outlets who stand by to send this message around the world.

He smooths his hair and takes a deep breath. He started his career as a reporter, but for the past ten or more years has been a producer on the other side of the camera. *But I'll do whatever's required for TJ.* He sends a silent message to her: *Hang in there. We're trying to find you.*

A ding on his phone indicates a text. He looks down, and it's NCI, ready to go.

"Okay, the network is ready," he shouts to those in the room. "Everyone quiet, please. Porter, up here with me. Be ready to talk when I tell you."

The chatter ceases, and the air becomes still. Roger dials a number on his phone and adjusts his wireless earpiece. "I'm getting the control room on the line." He listens, then says, "Count me down." He wipes a bead of sweat from his upper lip. He listens again, then barks, "We're going live in 30 seconds."

He squeezes his eyes shut, opens them again, and takes a sip from his water bottle. He picks up a microphone, takes a deep breath, looks directly into the camera and waits.

"Thank you, Geri. I am reporting live from Prague in the Czech Republic, where we have been looking for one of our colleagues who was kidnapped four days ago by members of a suspected sex trafficking organization.

"TJ Banks is a long-time and well-respected freelance reporter and videographer who has covered major crimes including many sex trade operations in the United States and around the world. She was covering one such bust in Bucharest, Romania when we believe she was taken against her will."

He waves Porter into the shot, now dressed in his dark jacket, white shirt and dark tie. Roger notices a light sheen of perspiration on his face. "With us is Agent Aaron Porter of the FBI. Agent Porter, what can you add?"

Porter stands beside Lester, who points the mic toward him, and looks at the camera. "The Federal Bureau of Investigation is working closely with law enforcement agencies in Europe to search for and find Ms. Banks. We are doing everything in our power to seek out those who took her and may be holding her captive. We believe her last location was in Jablonec, Czech Republic but she could be in Poland, Slovakia, Hungary or the surrounding area by now.

"The people who kidnapped Ms. Banks are armed and very dangerous. Do not approach them but call the FBI or your local law enforcement agency if you have any information." He looks back to Lester and nods.

Roger Lester continues. "As the image on your screen indicates, TJ Banks is 5 feet 9, has short dark hair and was wearing a bullet-proof vest marked PRESS when she was taken, like this one." He holds up his Kevlar covering for a moment. "NCI is offering a $100-thousand dollar reward for the person who has information on her whereabouts or knows something about the people holding her. As Agent Porter said, please contact the FBI or your local police. We will keep you updated on the search."

He pauses for a beat, and in a shaky voice says, "TJ, if you hear this, we *will* find you."

He straightens his shoulders. "Reporting live from Prague, I'm Roger Lester for NCI."

He stands for a few more moments looking at the camera until a signal in his ear tells him he is off the air. His shoulders slump and he lets out a sigh of relief.

"Well done." Agent Porter puts his hand on Roger's shoulder. "I know... how much she means to you."

"Thanks." Roger makes direct eye contact and in the agent's gaze he detects a momentary flash of deep concern. *And to you as well.*

"The heat is on. We'll squeeze 'em out," Roger says, his jaw set.

Chapter 103

The stinging, throbbing pain from my body force my eyes to pop open. Or maybe it was the sound of the door opening that awakens me.

It's dark in the room, but a hallway light behind the person at the door silhouettes Darkmover wearing what looks like a shiny, long-sleeved robe.

She pads in slowly and silently until she stands beside the bed.

"Please… don't hurt me. What do you want?" My voice sounds weak, submissive. The former TJ Banks would be disgusted by the sound, but the current one is just thinking about staying alive.

"Ahh, my dear, you are awake." She reaches out and runs her hand through my short hair. "Vee must let your hair grow. Men prefer long hair."

"I… please… I promise—"

"You promise? You are a fast learner. Zhat ees good."

"What do I need to—?"

"Oh, my dear, you do not need to do anything right now."

Darkmover pulls the bow of her cloth belt and the robe drops to the floor, revealing her naked body. "Just relax…"

"Nooo…." The word comes out of me softly, resigned.

Darkmover crawls into the bed beside me. I squeeze my eyes shut as her hand roams over my body.

Chapter 104

Aaron Porter surveys the room in Prague where U.S. and Europe agents are fielding phone calls, gathering information.

Leads are coming in from all over Europe in response to Lester's live report.

But are any of them credible? Will we get a tip as to where TJ is being held?

"Boss. That cyber investigator from L.A. on line two for you."

Aaron nods at his colleague and takes a seat at a desk with a phone. "Agent Porter."

"This is Cho Zhang, friend of TJ Banks. I have information for you."

"Thanks for calling. Just a moment." Porter looks for Roger Lester. "Lester! It's Cho." Lester rushes over.

"I've got you on speaker. What do you have?"

"I reach friend of Gabriel's in Prague. He has network of dark web contacts and they believe they locate area where TJ may be. It is in Bratislava, capital of Slovakia, near the Danube River."

Porter looks at Roger, whose face is lit with excitement. Lester has pulled open a map on his cell phone and is searching for the area.

"That's excellent, Ms. Zhang. I'll gather my team and head that way."

"I will have more specific location information for you shortly." A pause. "You must find my friend," she adds softly. "Especially after what they do to Gabriel."

The sadness radiating from the woman is profound, even through the telephone line.

"We will do everything we can. And we appreciate your help."

Roger Lester brings up the map of Bratislava on a larger computer screen, and Porter joins him.

"That's three hours by car from here," Lester says. "Or we could fly into Vienna and it's an hour drive from there. Probably faster that way. How fast can you get an airplane?"

"We don't have aircraft at our disposal, Lester. Let me see—"

"Never mind." *That's the best you can do?!* Roger is peeved by his bureaucratic tone. "I'll have NCI rent a helicopter, which will be even quicker. Get two of your top people and be ready to roll."

Chapter 105

I'm going to be sick.

Bile rises in my throat as Darkmover runs a finger from my cheek to my chin to my chest and to my stomach. While the thought flashes in my mind of spewing an Exorcist stream of green vomit directly into this woman's revolting face, I imagine what the resulting punishment would be, and it stops me. I gulp.

Her hand goes lower. Down my thigh. To my knee. And back up to where my legs are splayed, held in place solidly against the four-poster bed.

My eyes open wide. *No! This can't be happening! This monster... this woman who has herded women into prisons to be assaulted and beaten and drugged... is raping me!*

And what the hell are these feelings? Am I aroused by it?! How can that be? That is not possible! I hate what she is doing... But tingles of pleasure expand as she gently touches around my vagina, then softly massages my clitoris, then plunges two fingers into me... *I have to stop this!* "Nooo!"

"Eet is all right, my dear. See, you are responding just as you should." Her fingers pull out of me and she slides my wetness down my cheek and into her mouth. "Velcome to zee family." Her fingers go back down and into me, then she kisses me on the cheek. She slides her mouth over and plunges her tongue in mine.

I'm so shocked by it all—her being here, the sensations, her touches, her disgusting kiss—I am frozen in place. *This can't be happening! I can't let it go on! I—*

I clamp my teeth down on her tongue.

Darkmover screeches and pulls back. "You stupid girl," she hisses. With that, she takes her fingernails and scrapes them hard across my stomach. With her other hand, she slaps my face, over and over again. "Nicholas!" she shouts as she stands up, pulling on her robe.

A man comes to the door. "Yes?" he says in a low voice.

"Eet ees your turn." Her voice is stony. "But no drugs zees time. Vee need to teach zees girl how to behave."

With that Ileana "Darkmover" Barrionuevo leaves the room and I'm alone with the man.

I have nothing to fight back with.

The man named Nicholas is the tall one I stabbed in the basement the other day. *Or when was that? What day is it? I have lost all track of time.*

A gauze bandage covers the lower part of Nicholas' jaw and he has a dark, sadistic look on his face.

I remember one sex trafficking victim, rescued after she was arrested in a police raid, who said, "First you need to escape your own mind, right?"

I tell myself to go to a different place in my brain.

After Darkmover molested—no, raped—me, my body's shocking reaction to the stimulus, and now this man forcing himself on me, I tell my brain to conjure up Venice Beach, with the powerful ocean waves roaring in, slipping out, crashing in again. Repeat over and over. *Concentrate on the crashing surf and the soft air and the warm sun. That's all you need to think about. It will soon be over.*

And soon it was. Nicholas doesn't apparently perform well unless his victim is resisting. He finally crawls off me and leaves the room.

I fall asleep to the imagined sea sounds in my head.

Chapter 106

Roger Lester is strapped into one of the Bell JetRanger's seats with Agent Aaron Porter, two of his men and the pilot, cruising at 144 mph.

We're on our way, TJ. Hang in there just a little longer. We'll find you!

Roger repeats that over and over in his head like a mantra. He can't let himself think the unthinkable. Somehow, they *will* locate her. If it's not too late.

It's 204 miles from Prague to Bratislava, and the helicopter's pilot says they can easily do that on one tank of gas. They should be there in about an hour. Roger checks the implant's tracking screen. Nothing. He sees Porter glance over at him.

"It's pure science fiction. Don't you get that?" Porter says.

"What are you talking about?"

"The implant. I know you're putting all your hopes on it, but guys I talked to says those devices are a sham."

Roger scowls at the agent. "Care to enlighten me?"

"First of all, they say a tiny device like that couldn't be read by more than a couple hundred meters with no interference in the way. So, no way would a satellite pick it up."

Roger considers that. "What else?"

"IF we got close to it, several substances could cloud or block the signal, such as metal, concrete and other solid materials. In addition, water is a major barrier for radio frequency, and because the human body is mostly made up of water, it would also dull the signal."

Roger is silent. "You've got your intel. This is all I have." He looks back down and continues to stare at the screen.

Darkmover's face scrunches up in a scowl as she glowers at the computer.

Her satellite phone and internal message machine have been pinging for the past couple of hours with the news stories from NCI.

"Nicholas!" she shouts, and the tall man rushes to her side.

"Vhat is going on? Vhy all these messages?"

"Eet ees zee American. There are news reports of her being missing."

"*Futu-i!* (Fuck!)" she barks.

"Should we move her again?" Nicholas asks.

"No, not yet. Let me make a call." She dismisses him with her hand and reaches for her cell.

The sound of the dreaded phone buzzes in Charles Wilcox's desk.

It's been such a pleasure not to hear that disgusting Romanian voice for so many days. Charles thought he was done with her for good.

Until now.

He secures his office door, then unlocks the center drawer of his desk and reaches for the vibrating burner phone. He takes a big breath and opens it. He starts to open his mouth but shuts it when he hears "Charles!" loud in his ear.

"Yes?" he says timidly.

"You bastard, vhat are you doing? You vere supposed to call off the FBI, and here they are on my tail!"

Wilcox blinks a couple of times. *What is she talking about? How did the FBI—?*

"I don't understand what… I mean, you have the reporter. What is going on?"

"Don't you watch the fucking news? Ees everywhere! Stories about her kidnapping. You need to stop those damned FBI agents *now!*" she roars.

Wilcox closes his eyes. *He thought it was too good to be true. He had hoped Darkmover would get rid of that damned woman and he could go back to his—*

"Are you listening to me?!" Darkmover / Illeana screams. "Eef you do not call off those dogs now, you vill end up on the bottom of the river!"

Wilcox shoves his thumb into his mouth and chews on the nail. "Um… They were never supposed… yes, I will contact them right away."

"You better do more than that!" she hisses. "If they are not directed back to the United States in 10 minutes, I will send my people after you!" She ends the call before he can say another word.

He bites his nails while he thinks. He boasted to her earlier that he could call off the FBI, but he never thought he would ever have to do it.

But instead of making a phone call, Wilcox gathers up the three phones in his desk, takes a few files and leaves his office.

Aaron Porter's cell buzzes in his coat pocket, next to his shoulder holster carrying a 9mm Glock.

It's Cho.

He shouts over the deafening noise in the chopper. "Cho, it's Porter! What do you have?"

"We believe she is being held at a sewage disposal plant on the southern outskirts of Bratislava. On Orechová Cesta Street. Address and coordinates coming on PGP line."

Roger leans over, expectantly. The noise from the chopper almost drowns out Porter's voice.

"Good work. We should be there in about 25 minutes."

"I have team who can be there in 10. Should I send them?"

Porter looks at his watch. He runs a hand over his head. "No. I mean, yes, yes, send them, but just to surveil the area, see if they can determine her exact location and make sure Darkmover or his people don't leave with TJ."

"Okay." She disconnects the line.

"We have a location!" Porter shouts to Roger. He looks at his phone and the coordinates come in. He shows them to the pilot, who nods and inputs them into his navigation equipment.

Porter tosses a mint in his mouth, the strong flavor shooting an intense icy coldness through his sinus passages and mouth.

TJ, we're almost there.

Chapter 107

There's increased activity outside the door, louder than I've heard since I've been here.

What is going on? Are we moving again? I try my restraints, but they don't budge.

Damn it, think! The implant isn't working, the earrings with the tracking device are gone, so you're on your own. Come on, TJ, no more pity party! Don't just lie there, you've got to do something to get out of here! There are girls to be saved. You can't let them down!

"Hey! Someone! I need to go to the bathroom!" I shout as loud as I can. "Please! Someone!"

The door opens and deChantal/Cheryl slips in, a wild look on her face.

"What's going on out there?" I ask.

"I'm not sure. Something's happening, and Ileana is not happy about it, but I can't tell what it's about."

"Look, I really have to go to the bathroom. Can you please untie me?"

"Well, I don't think I…" Cheryl's brows furrow, conflicted.

"Please! They'll get angry if I pee all over this mattress and they'll blame you."

That gets Cheryl's attention. She takes off the ties and I sit up, fighting dizziness. "Thanks. Look, I've got to try to get out of here. If you come with me, I can help you get back to Alabama or wherever you want to go. Out of this life. What do you say?"

"Oh no, that's impossible, you…"

"Cheryl, you don't want to be a slave to these people for the rest of what will probably be a very short life, do you?! Now where's the closest way out?"

I slip on the red robe and tie it tight around my waist. I stuff two of the lengths of restraint rope in a pocket, give one to Cheryl and keep the other in my hand. "Use this as a weapon. Snap it in someone's face or twist it around their neck."

Cheryl is wide-eyed for a moment. Then she pulls the rope with both hands, realizing. "Uh, the only doors are on either ends of the hallway, but we'll never get that far."

"What about a window?"

She perks up. "There's a window in room 8 right next to us."

"Great! Okay, stay calm, look out the door and if it's clear, we'll both walk quickly there."

Cheryl nods. She opens the door slowly, looks both ways, and pulls her head back in. I can hear scraping sounds of furniture being moved, shouting in some Slovak type of language, general chaos down at the end of the hall. "I don't think they'll see us. Come on."

She leads the way out, and as nonchalantly as possible with my heart pounding in my chest, we inch along the wall, open the next room's door and hurry in, closing it behind us.

To see a man and a woman having rough sex on a small, dirty bed.

The woman, her long red hair strewn on the bare pillow, looks at us in shock then, with her eyes, pleads for help. The man is oblivious to our presence and continues his thrusting.

I motion to Cheryl that I will wrap my rope around the man's neck, and she should take his hands. On the silent count of three, I strangle the man while Cheryl grabs his wrists and tries to bind them behind him. The man's eyes go wide, but he can't make any more than a muffled sound. He thrashes about for a very long couple of minutes until his air is gone and he collapses on the bed. I help Cheryl tie his hands, then cover him up with a blanket on the bed and signal to the redhead to come with us.

Her eyes dart madly around the room. She grabs a gown and pulls it over her head.

The window slides up.

◎

Chapter 108

Roger looks at his phone's clock: seven minutes until they touch down in Bratislava.

I just hope she's still there. The empty feeling in the pit of his stomach reminds him of the last failed attempt to find TJ.

He glances out the chopper's window, a brilliant green landscape below, with a river boat slowly sailing down the Danube River. *There are people laughing, drinking, enjoying themselves on that ship, with no idea of the atrocities happening just a few miles away. They are—*

The vibration of the phone in his hand ends that thought. There's an alert. He opens the screen and a wide grin spreads over his face.

"So much for your so-called science fiction." Roger shows the phone to Porter who raises his eyebrows in disbelief and gives a thumbs up.

TJ's implant tracking device once again blinks a bright green steady pattern.

On Aaron Porter's instructions, the helicopter lands in a field a half a mile from the sewage plant, to minimize the sound giving away their arrival.

Cho's team of four meets Porter, Lester and his two men. *Not a big show of force, but it will have to do.* The rest of his team are on their way, but it could be an hour or more before they arrive.

And Porter's not waiting another minute.

He quickly assesses the fire power between the seven of them, as Lester is unarmed. Porter pulls a small caliber pistol from an ankle holster and hands it to Roger.

"You know how to use this?"

Roger takes it, expertly pops out the ammunition magazine, sees it is full and pops it back in. He tests the sight by pointing the weapon down and away from Porter. "Got it." He tucks it away in the small of his back.

They hand out clip-on walkie-talkies, form a plan and start jogging toward the sewage plant and TJ's location.

Chapter 109

My body aches, but I slither out the window and lower myself to the ground, then help the other two women get out.

The smell of sewage is strong in the warm air. We hug the side of the concrete building, and it's cool on my back and arms.

"Cheryl, where are we? What city is this?"

She smiles brightly. "This is Bratislava."

At my perplexed look, Cheryl adds, "Slovakia. It's a beautiful little town. Sometimes they take me to The Church of the Seven Sorrows."

I turn to the redhead. "I'm TJ. What's your name?"

She shakes her head. "No Englees."

A local accent.

"*Nasov*," Cheryl says. Name.

"Ahh, Michelle."

"Your Slovakian name?" I ask.

The woman gives a shy smile. "Dalka."

I nod. "That's pretty."

The grass is damp and soothing to my bare feet as we stay close to the side of the building, inching our way from the escape window. Some distance away a chain-link fence topped with barbed wire surrounds us. *That's going to be tough to climb over.* On either side of the metal barrier is thick shrubbery and trees.

We reach the end of the building, and I peer around the edge of the structure. A solitary man is standing guard, smoking a cigarette. I hold my hand back to indicate the girls should stop.

"Cheryl, you step out as 'deChantal' and smile and wave the guy over this way," I whisper. "Make sure he comes right here, and I will jump him and we'll tie him up. Can you explain to Dalka that's what we're doing?"

"Okay." Cheryl speaks to the redhead in a Slovak language, guttural and nothing that I can understand. The woman's eyes go wide but she nods in acknowledgement.

Feigning a sexy demeanor, deChantal strolls out from the side of the building and calls out. "Oh, *vojak!* (soldier)" she says, waving at the man. He looks around in confusion, then walks cautiously toward Cheryl.

He says something to her, but Cheryl just keeps smiling seductively, indicating with her hand for him to come her way.

As soon as he clears the corner, I spring into action, rushing him from behind. I quickly wrap the length of rope around his burly neck and pull tight. His arms flail around him, and he tries to pull at the cord, but can't get his fingers under it. His resistance slows, and I continue cutting off his air until he slumps to the ground, unconscious. We tie his hands behind him and race toward the protection of the foliage at the edge of the property.

The fencing is rusted in places, but otherwise secure. "We're going to have to find a section we can break through."

Pounding feet in the distance somewhere behind us forces me to stop in my tracks. "They're coming after us! That way!" I motion to the women to follow, and we run along the perimeter of the sewage disposal plant, away from the sound, and hide in a thick section of bushes.

Aaron Porter puts up a hand to signal a slowdown.

They're at the edge of the property where they believe TJ is being held, but it's surrounded by large trees and thick brush. Not to mention prison-style razor wire on top of metal fencing.

"Anyone have something to cut this fence with?" he asks in a loud whisper. One of Cho's men unzips a long duffle-type bag and pulls out a red-handled pair of large snippers. Porter takes them and starts slicing through the chain link.

Suddenly there's a strange metallic sound coming from barely 25 yards from us.

"We've got to move!" I take off running again, this time along a paved pathway toward the center of the property. We pass more than half a dozen huge round reservoirs filled with water until the sound disappears behind us. We dash back toward the safety of the foliage covered fence and continue towards what we hope will be a way out.

Vehicles. A half dozen of them, and no one around.

It's been a long time since I've hot-wired a car. High school to be exact, when my so-called boyfriend decided he wanted to go for a joy ride in his neighbors' Mustang. *Can I remember which wires need to go together?*

If it works, where we're going, I'm not sure, but my main thought is very far away from these monsters.

Chapter 110

Aaron Porter leads the men as they squeeze through the sheared section of the fence, pushing their way through the bushes.

Staying along the perimeter, in the foliage, they cautiously move toward the first building they see.

"Porter!" Lester whispers into the walkie-talkie.

Porter, in the lead, turns back to look at him.

Lester holds up the implant app on his phone. The red blinking light, which has been stationary for the last half hour, is now traveling.

"She's on the move, away from here!"

Porter looks at the screen, surveys the surrounding area. "And she's traveling fast. They may be transporting her in a vehicle again."

The mission to take down Darkmover versus the mission to rescue TJ. What is the greater good? What will affect more people?

Capturing one of the biggest sex traffickers and potentially rescuing scores of women held against their will is certainly the greater impact.

But the pang in Porter's chest tells him finding TJ Banks is his top priority.

"We're splitting up," Porter commands. "The six of you continue to surveil the area to infiltrate Darkmover's operation." He checks his watch. "Wait until the rest of the crew arrives, which should be in about 30 minutes. Lester and I are going after the subject."

The men nod and continue toward the first white building with a red roof.

Porter gestures that Lester come with him. "Let's get back to the chopper. We'll have a better chance of catching up with them."

Lester shakes his head. "She's not that far away. I'm going on foot." He takes off running before Porter can argue.

Porter goes back through the slit in the fence and sprints toward the helicopter.

It works, and I get the engine started of a small silver foreign vehicle.

We hop in the car, me in the driver's seat, Cheryl next to me and Dalka in the back.

Our pupils are huge from adrenaline, and if we were hooked up to a monitor, our combined heartbeats would surely thump like a marching band.

I resist the urge to speed through the narrow driveway, but try to drive normally, not like someone would who has been kidnapped, held prisoner, raped and is now escaping from her captors.

A glance in the rear-view mirror. A man is running after us—with a gun!

I reach the edge of the sewage complex property and hit the gas.

Roger Lester's blinking tracking device matches the small silver auto driving ahead of him.

She's in that car! He draws his weapon and increases his running speed. Moments later, the vehicle takes off like a shot and disappears down the street.

"Damn it!" Lester stops and activates the comm device. "Porter! They took off, fast. Come pick me up at the north edge of the property!"

Wait, do I drive on the right or left side of the road?

Last time I rented a car in Europe, I was in the UK and found myself driving on the "wrong" side of the road. But this car has the steering wheel on the left like those in the U.S., and so right side it is. I floor it.

Cheryl braces herself against the dashboard, and in my mind's eye I can imagine Dalka hanging on for dear life in the back seat.

I zip along the edge of the town, looking for any signage that indicates a major freeway to get as far away from Darkmover. Then I can find a phone and contact Aaron and Roger and they'll come for—

The *thup-thup-thup* of a helicopter's gyrating rotors sounds like it's right on top of us.

"What is that?" Cheryl asks, trying to see the aircraft.

"I'm not sure… it might be…" *Could it be Aaron and Roger? No, it's probably more of Darkmover's thugs, as she's pulling out all the stops to catch—*

There's a voice from a loudspeaker above them. "This is the FBI. Pull your vehicle over."

What?! Could it… but how do I know? I can't risk—

"TJ! It's Roger. It's okay. Pull over!"

Tears spill out and down my cheeks when I hear Roger's sweet, friendly voice.

They found me!

Chapter 111

I breathe a huge sigh of relief when Aaron Porter's team finally takes down Darkmover in Bratislava.

She and her criminal cohorts will be in Romanian prisons for a long time.

Charles Wilcox from the Office of Refugee Resettlement is in the wind, but Porter found and shut down his accounts in the Cayman Islands. Porter guesses he is laying low somewhere internationally, and figures Wilcox will resurface when he needs money.

Meanwhile, the FBI arrests a man Wilcox was working with, Bernardo Serafin, aka "BS," a former pimp and one of the men running the Phoenix migrant house. His so-called nonprofit called Foundation for Fostering Immigrants was a front for Serafin who would "donate" to causes close to border patrol and ICE agents when they move two to three children at a time his way. It was all under the guise of putting them in small foster homes, but instead they'd be placed in his sex trafficking homes.

To the children, he'd say their parents were sent back to their home country—which often was true—so they could no longer come get them. That was also true because once they were in his FFI system, the kids would never be found. He'd tell them, "We are your new family now."

Last thing I heard, Serafin is singing like a proverbial canary and spilling info on Wilcox.

The FBI, Homeland Security, DHHS and other agencies reunite more than 100 children with their parents but are still working to recover potentially more than 250 still "lost" in the system.

I locate a little one-bedroom vacation rental on the south shore of Kauai, Hawaii.

On the recommendation of just about everyone, with which I eventually concur, I take some time off to heal, regroup, think.

The beach is just a few steps away from the little condo, and instead of jumping rope, these days I walk over every morning with a cup of coffee to watch the sunrise, catch a turtle bobbing in the surf, feel the sun on my face, and just be. I'm not used to doing nothing, but my body and mind make the decision for me, and for the first time in a very long time, I'm beginning to relax and appreciate life in the moment I'm in right now.

Both Roger and Aaron want to come visit, but I'm not ready. My mind is still muddled when it comes to the two of them, and I don't want to be rushed into any big decisions. I invite Cho to come, telling her she can work her cyber investigations from anywhere. She says she'll think about it, but I know she won't, as she's such a homebody.

Aaron Porter's life is calmer these days since shutting down Darkmover.

He sells his house in Albuquerque and moves into a small New York apartment to take a lateral, permanent transfer to the Bureau's Child Exploitation and Human Trafficking Task Force.

There's much less drama in his life without TJ, although he also knows something significant is missing. But he's a patient man. He can wait.

Roger Lester is back in Atlanta, working daily for NCI.

He's not able to convince TJ to keep a few clothing items at his place for when she's ready to go back to work. But she agrees to keep the CZ earrings and he's happy they are in her ears when he sees her off at the Vienna Airport. He also notices she is not wearing the diamond necklace from a previous boyfriend that used to be such a part of her.

Every day Roger opens the earring tracking app to see where she is. The blinking red dot brings him some consolation when it comes to their relationship, and with that simple act, he feels closer to her.

I still haven't made a decision about what's next for me.

The relentless pounding of the surf calms and grounds me. As I sit on the warm sand, sunshine caressing my face, soft breezes teasing my hair, questions swirl through my brain.

Do I keep freelancing, shooting crime and trauma around the country and continue my nomadic life? It's been my lifestyle for so many years, it's practically ingrained in my DNA. And I am good at what I do.

Or do I take the NCI job and settle down in one place? Get a great apartment, and focus on getting a real life after work hours?

What about going after sex traffickers? It is still high on my list, but at the moment, I shudder when I think about what happened when it led me to Darkmover.

Should I find out what a tumultuous yet exciting relationship I might have with Aaron? Or try a safer, deeper one with Roger?

It's still too early for any of that yet.

But soon perhaps.

No. One decision is definite. My resolve is greater than ever to rid the world of the evil that is sex trafficking of women and children, despite what I know is a temporary trepidation.

My search for Charles Wilcox will never end until he's put behind bars. I also vow to find Katrina and hope it's not too late.

And I *will* get my own life back again.

The End

Request for Review

If you enjoyed this book, please consider leaving an honest review
on my book page on Amazon.com.
Simply go to Amazon.com/author/lauriefagen.
Or search for "*Raw Image* by Laurie Fagen,"
click on the book image, then scroll down to "Review this Product"
and click on the "Write a customer review" button.

Your comments need not be long,
a couple of sentences will do, along with your chosen star rating.

This is one of the most valuable things
you can do to support an author.
Thank you so much for your consideration!

Acknowledgments

While writers often work in solitude, we typically rely on a variety of experts to assist with details that make a novel richer.

I want to recognize and give my great gratitude to Red Light Rebellion, a prevention organization that educates young people about the dangers of child sex trafficking and empowers them to fight injustice, all for no charge. Run by the husband and wife team of Breanna and Brendon, Breanna started it during her senior year in high school after learning her age group was the primary target for sex trafficking. Info: redlightrebellion.org.

Another very useful site while writing this story was the National Human Trafficking Hotline at www.humantraffickinghotline.org/en along with the FBI Phoenix website, which was very helpful for local color. A variety of online spy shops helped me write about the GPS earrings and RFID implant.

My thanks to Kirby Plessas, with Curious Kirby Creatives on Facebook and Plessas Experts, Inc., a cyber guru in internet investigations and training, and good friend, who assisted with much of the deep and dark web details; Timothy W. Moore, retired Phoenix Police officer as well as Tyler Service, a current Chandler Police officer for assistance with police procedural; and Marco Conelli, a former undercover detective with the NYPD, whom I met at a Writers' Police Academy. Turns out all three are also fellow musicians!

I covered the crime beat for KWWL-TV, an NBC affiliate television station in Waterloo, IA, and am grateful for personnel I met from the local police and sheriff's departments, courts, jails and other entities dealing with criminal behavior.

I so appreciate my good friend Dale Dexter, a videographer with whom I worked at KWWL, who helped with the latest video camera details; and my longtime and dear friend Pam Hildebrand Grimes, another KWWL co-worker, who retired from WGN in Chicago, for providing camera technology and current terminology.

My hat is off to Ann Videan of Videan Unlimited, an editor, author and book shepherd, for her formatting expertise, sharp eye, and longtime friendship.

As always, I want to recognize my Mystery Critique Writing Group of Anna Bartkowski, Margaret Morse, Karen Randau and Sandy Wright for their great ideas and longtime friendship.

I rely on beta readers for their input, so thanks to Sheila Roe, Katrina Shawver, Jane Shea Degnan, Margaret Morse and Karen Randau for your great catches and suggestions.

My sincere appreciation goes once again to eagle eye proofreader Sandy Vernon Gates.

I placed my fictional character, Katrina, in Bitburg, Germany, where my late husband went to the military high school there while his father was a JAG in the Air Force.

Thank you to Roxana Dragomir, a Romanian speaker, who helped confirm Google Translate, and Elena Thornton for referring me to her.

And *mahalo* (thank you) to Kauai, my home away from home, for the setting for TJ's recovery at the end of *Raw Image*.

Character Names

And thanks to the readers who won the opportunity to have their names in this novel!

"Barbie," the young mother from the mall shooting, comes from Patreon member Barbara R. Hopkins in Maine.

"Eva," "Barbie's" daughter, comes from the name of Patty and James' daughter in Chandler.

"Chun Chinese," the Asian eatery in Venice Beach, is so named for my dear friend and fellow writer Jessica Chun Williams of Venice Beach.

I used writer Sheila Roe's name for Maricopa County Assistant District Attorney "Sheila Roe."

"Katrina" is TJ Banks' high school friend she believes has been trafficked, named after writer and friend Katrina Shawver.

From the drawing at d'Vine Gourmet, Chandler:

Jackie Sereno's last name is used for the police officer "L. Sereno" at the Albuquerque mall shooting.

Ross Hamilton's first name is used for the young production assistant, "Ross," who helps TJ find the mall shooter's car.

Darkmover's real name is "Ileana," from Ileana Barrionuevo.

From Ocotillo Women's League (OWLs), March 2022:

Toni Flanagan of OWL and Rachel Karls-Gomes, a fellow Sonoran Arts League member, become the FBI agent in Phoenix "Toni Karls."

Kathy Wilcox's last name is one of the bad guys, "Charlie Wilcox."

Cheryl Morgan and deChantal Riley become the names of a trafficked woman TJ befriends and helps escape whose real name is "Cheryl," but the traffickers have named her "deChantal."

From VUU Page Turners Book Club in Chandler:

The woman in Darkmover's Bratislava warehouse becomes "Irene" for Irene Rosenthal.

Johnnie Godfrey becomes NCI VP "Steven Godfrey."

From JK Books and Gifts in Earlham, IA:

Albuquerque police officer "Buzz Cut Worsold" is named after Denise Worsold.

"Geri," the NCI anchor, is named after Geri Williamson, the late wife of John Williamson.

From Payson Book Fest 2022:

"Veronica," TJ's "new name" with trafficker Darkmover, is from Veronica Freeland.

The pimp "Serafin" who helped Charlie Wilcox is named for Charlie Serafin.

From Grand Canyon Writers Sept. 22:

FBI Agent Aaron Porter's team member "Ormerod" in Romania is named for Jayne Ormerod.

About the Author

Laurie Fagen is a long-time "writer by habit" who has written for radio and television news; corporate video, films and documentaries; magazines and newspapers; and now fiction novels.

An honorable mention in Alfred Hitchcock Mystery Magazine's Mysterious Photograph short story contest and a life-long love of reading whodunits led to multiple published short stories in Sisters in Crime and other anthologies, four full-length novels, two novellas and multiple short stories.

Following a career in broadcast news, Fagen published a Chandler, AZ community newspaper with her late husband, Geoff Hancock for 13 years. She is also a fiber and jewelry artist and occasional classic jazz singer, and lives in Chandler, AZ with her two rescue cats.

Info: www.ReadLaurieFagen.com

Coming Soon

Mental Image

Book #2 in the new "Behind the Lens Mysteries"

TJ Banks, a hardened freelance news reporter/videographer, has been covering major national crimes and exposing sex trafficking, until she herself is kidnapped, brutally raped and sex trafficked.

She struggles to recover from the horrific incidents. Despite the trauma, she must navigate a path forward and is determined to rebuild her life and career. Coming in 2026.

Excerpt:

Sharp pain. Agony.

The coarse rope around my wrists and ankles, tied to the metal bed posts, cut into my skin as I struggle to get free.

I yell for help, but no one comes.

I curse my captors, but there's only silence.

I sob, broken, not knowing when or if I will ever be freed.

Then rough hands grab my arms, my legs, my breasts, my face and I thrash to avoid them, but to no avail.

I scream again and wake myself up from yet another nightmare.

I sit up in bed, my pulse racing. The blue digital bedside clock numbers read 3:42 a.m. I realize I'm in my vacation rental condo in Poipu, on the south shore of Kauai, Hawaii. The crashing waves from the ocean a few steps away begin to still my pounding heart.

It's over. You're not in danger. Everything's fine. I repeat this like a mantra, over and over again, and I wonder if I'll ever believe it.

The full moon pours its white light through my bedroom window, and I pad across the room to look out. *Breathe in, breathe out. Breathe in, breathe out.* Just like my therapist, Maluhia, a lovely "kupuna," or elder in the islands, teaches me how to calm myself in our twice-weekly sessions.

Maluhia's been working with me to come to terms with being kidnapped and brutally raped by sex traffickers, and hard work it has been.

I just start to think I'm ready to move forward, get back to my life, when a memory, a smell, a sound takes me to my knees again. I'm disgusted with myself for being here for more than three months, not knowing why I can't simply "snap" out of it.

But like Maluhia, Roger—my former "friend with benefits," colleague and co-worker who helped rescue me from that Romanian hell—gently advises me it will take time.

Then there's Aaron, the FBI special agent who recently relocated to New York City with whom I've had an on-again, off-again relationship. He's been less communicative, but it's probably because I'm reticent about my plans.

Because there are no plans. There's no timeline. No goals. Nothing. Nada.

And that drives me crazy, so I can only imagine how Roger and Aaron feel.

I go to the kitchen for a glass of water, and take it out on the lanai, settling in a rocking chair facing the ocean. A soft breeze stirs my now shoulder length hair, which is growing out from the short spikes I've worn for years, and long enough that it tickles my cheeks.

A tiny "mew" interrupts my reverie. I look around to find the sound, and the moon casts its reflection on a skinny gray calico cat standing at the edge of my tiny yard.

"Oh, you're back, are you?" I put my hand out and beckon with a wiggle of my fingers, but I know the feral feline won't come near. "I haven't seen you for a few days. I guess we've both got trust issues in common."

The cat doesn't respond, but sits, and begins licking its leg.

"Yeah, story of my life. I think just maybe I'd be here long enough to have a pet. Then you turn up. But you're just a wild child." *Something else we have in common.*

I rock a few more minutes and watch the cat grooming itself. I get up from the chair, but the slight squeak and movement startles the animal, causing it to bolt off in a flash.

"Sorry, cat." I look around the yard but don't see it. "Hey, that's a good name for you: Bolt."

I hope you come back.

Other Books by Laurie Fagen

Equalizer
In e-book

Young radio reporter Lisa Powers has a nose for news, but sometimes makes reckless decisions when it comes to covering the crime beat.

Lisa reports on a shocking homicide that halts a white-collar money-laundering trial but finds herself facing down the killer. She hunts for the murderer of a Jane Doe found in the desert decades ago that may have something to do with a Native American moccasin maker.

There's a smell of death in her "Haunted Hallows" mystery theatre podcast, leading to yet another mystery to be solved. Prequel novella in "Behind the Mic Mysteries."

Fade Out
In print, e-book and audio book

The first full-length crime fiction novel in the series of "Behind the Mic Mysteries," Lisa Powers covers a massive fire which destroys the opulent mansion of a reclusive pharmaceutical heir, and her career is jeopardized when the story gets way too hot.

From the dark streets of the metro Phoenix area to the peaceful red rocks of Sedona, Lisa dodges bullets investigating the cold case of a kidnapped bank executive found murdered and discovers horrors she never imagined while tracking down a missing father.

She finds herself facing down criminals in addition to reporting on them. Book #1.

Dead Air
In print, e-book and audio book

In Fagen's second full-length crime fiction novel, young radio crime reporter Lisa Powers covers a double cop shooting that tears the community apart, at the risk of her own emotional health.

Her cold case is a 1999 sexual assault involving a child, and Lisa is determined to help the now 19-year-old victim move forward with her life.

Lisa's "podcast," which she writes for fun at night after covering gritty crime stories during the day, is a film noir style story of a 1940s private eye and a dame. Only "L. N. Pane, P.I." is the dame, and a gentleman seeks help finding who is out to kill him. Book #2.

Bleeder
In print, e-book and audio book

In the third series novel, radio crime reporter Lisa Powers investigates a cold case and is close to discovering who gunned down a mom in her front yard – but in her drive to seek the truth, the killers find her first.

Lisa covers the court trial for the cop shooter who took her hostage, and now she must come face-to-face with him in court each day.

In Lisa's campy "Murder in the Air Mystery Theatre" podcast, there's a dead art gallery owner, a missing painting and plenty of suspects in "Art of the Steal."

www.ingramcontent.com/pod-product-compliance
Lightning Source LLC
Chambersburg PA
CBHW072107300726
48975CB00003B/743